DEDICATION

IN MEMORY OF MY MOTHER,
JANE MEADOWS OLIVER,
WHO ALWAYS HALVED HER PORTION WITH ME

London, England

Dearest Abigail,

It is so hard to believe you are gone. If I had not been at the harbor myself to tell you good-bye, I would have to pinch myself to believe my dearest friend in the entire world is in another world—the New World of America. I stayed and watched until the *Blessing* sailed out of sight.

You always were the first to try new things, but I never thought you would leave your homeland to travel to such an unknown land. I wish I shared your sense of adventure. But alas, my dear friend, my own dreams belong here in England.

Papa is not sure the Company exercised wisdom in sending Lieutenant Governor Sir Thomas Gates, Admiral George Somers, and Vice Admiral Captain Newport on the same ship—the *Sea Venture*. Papa is particularly fond of Admiral Somers, who he describes as a man of true character, giving and selfless. Papa says he has never known a nobler man and believes that if anyone can see this fleet of ships safely to Virginia, it is Admiral Somers.

Mother hugged the Rolfes good-bye. She thinks they are very brave to leave just now when Mistress Rolfe is pregnant with her first baby. Mother hopes the voyage will not be too much for her. At least they are on the *Sea Venture*. It will not pitch and roll so much as the smaller vessels. I am also comforted knowing that your family is together on the *Blessing,* and that your dear friends, the Pierces, traveled with you. That is, except for Captain Pierce. He is needed with the other leaders on the *Sea Venture.* Little Jane looks up to you so much. You must help her if she becomes afraid and misses her father on the journey.

John could not take his eyes off the six horses and two mares that the Captain ordered hoisted up in the air and over the edge of the pier onto the *Blessing.* You will have interesting company on your ship, my dear friend. One day you will be able to tell your grandchildren you sailed the seas with Virginia's first horses.

However, for the life of me, I cannot understand how Temperance Flowerdew is going to make it in the New World. She is such a scaredy-cat. Now I know you do not like her much, but she is one of the few girls your age, and you will need her company. With that in mind, I gave her a grand farewell as she boarded her ship, the *Falcon.*

Dear friend, I will not forget my solemn promise to pray for you every day and ask the Lord to watch over you and keep you safe. Now when you get this letter, you must not forget your solemn promise to me to tell me of all your adventures!

Your friend,

Elizabeth

We want to hear from you. Please send your comments about this book to us in care of zreview@zondervan.com. Thank you.

Zonder**kidz**®

The children's group of Zondervan

www.zonderkidz.com

Liberty Letters, The Personal Correspondence of Elizabeth Walton and Abigail Matthews
Copyright © 2003 by Nancy Oliver LeSourd

Map, from THE UNDERGROUND RAILROAD by Raymond Bial. Copyright © 1995 by Raymond Bial. Adapted and reprinted by permission of Houghton Mifflin Company. All Rights reserved.

Requests for information should be addressed to:
Grand Rapids, Michigan 49530

ISBN: 0-310-70351-4

Produced in association with the brand development agency of Evergreen Ideas, Inc., on behalf of Nancy LeSourd. For more information on Nancy LeSourd or the Liberty Letters series, visit www.Zonderkidz.com/libertyletters.

Editor: Gwen Ellis
Cover design: Michelle Lenger
Interior design: Tracey Moran
Photo layout design: Merit Alderink and Susan Ambs

Printed in the United States of America

03 04 05 06 07 /❖DC/ 10 9 8 7 6 5 4 3 2 1

Liberty Letters™

The personal correspondence of
Elizabeth Walton and Abigail Matthews

The Story of Pocahontas, 1613

Nancy LeSourd

Zonder**kidz**

Somewhere in the Atlantic Ocean

July 25, 1609

Dear Elizabeth,

This note must be short, and I do not know if you will ever have an opportunity to read it. But even if I am drowned, there is still a chance that this note could reach you. I want you to know that you have been my dearest friend ever, and I love you.

We are experiencing terrible gales and winds. The ship lists from side to side, and we are deathly afraid it will blow over. All hands are on deck—even Father—and he is not a sailor. I heard someone say it is a hurricane. If it is, we may all be doomed. Oh dearest Elizabeth, have I left my home and friends only to die on the way to my adventure? I must go. We are all needed to bail water.

Your friend forever, even in heaven,

Abigail

On Solid Ground in the Colony of Virginia

August 18, 1609

Dearest Elizabeth,

I must write this posthaste. Mother and Father and I are well—but many have been lost.

Several weeks into our journey, the sky darkened to a deep black. The wind increased and tossed the *Blessing* to and fro for three days. Our ship lost contact with all the others. The blackness of the night continued even into day as waves as high as the sky washed over the deck.

As the hull of the ship filled with water, women and children took buckets and scooped water and handed them to the next person in line. At the end of the line below the deck, one of the men lifted them up to the other men who threw the water overboard. All the men, whether they were sailors or not, had to report to the captain on the ship's deck. Our courageous captain instructed all of us in what to do. He never appeared frightened. But, dear Elizabeth, I was afraid.

Finally, the winds calmed down. We had not slept for three days, and we were all surprised that the *Blessing* was still afloat. We cheered our captain who, though weary, was much relieved. The captain told us that he and his men were working to rechart our course. It seems that Admiral Somers had given instructions as to what to do if the ships became separated. All the captains were to head to Bermuda, where they could meet up again.

A week after the winds calmed, the *Blessing* caught up with the *Lion* and the *Falcon*. I was ever so glad to see Temperance Flowerdew on the deck of the *Falcon*. The *Unity* was sore distressed—only the captain and one poor sailor were left alive. As the winds were strong for Virginia, the captains of the ships decided to head that way. We landed just one week ago. Yesterday, the *Diamond* and then the *Sparrow* docked. The *Sparrow* was barely afloat. There was great joy when we all were on the ground again, but our rejoicing was short-lived.

The wonderful new home we were all looking forward to is in great distress. Many of the people in the colony are sick—they call the summer months the "sickly time" as many suffer from disease. The colony is ill-prepared for so many new arrivals. There is precious little food or shelter. The bugs are horrible. I swat at my face and arms most of the day. It is hot and miserable. Father has spoken in hushed tones with Mother about the Indians as well.

I will write more soon.

Your friend,

Abigail

James Towne, Virginia

August 26, 1609

Dear Elizabeth,

We are hungry. The food we had on the ships spoiled from the seawater getting into it. We have no place to sleep but under the stars. Many are sick. The new leaders of the colony, with orders from the King, are on the *Sea Venture*, and it has not yet arrived. There is bickering among the leaders as to who will govern if the *Sea Venture* has been lost. With each week that passes, we grow more anxious about that ship.

Captain John Smith is furious with the so-called leaders, especially Captain Ratcliffe. He took men to Point Comfort to build a stockade. Others have been sent out to look for food.

I must close now. I hope you have heard word of the *Sea Venture* and that they are safe as well. Little Jane cries herself to sleep each night with worry about her father.

Your friend,

Abigail

London, England

August 27, 1609

Dearest Abigail,

I have been worried sick. I fear so for your life. Oh, how I hate to wait for news. I know that I may not hear from you soon—it could be months before a ship returns to London with your letters. I am just praying you made it there safely and that I will hear from you before too long. Mother tells me I should think good thoughts of you and not the worst, and so I will.

I will envision you on your grand adventure. I imagine the colonists there were quite happy to see all the ships arrive. What did they think of the horses? Where are you living? Did you find a wonderful home waiting for you? Papa told me that the leaders of James Towne all knew this third supply was coming, and so I am sure you are well provided for now. Please give my love to your dear parents, and know that I am thinking of you now in August, no matter when you actually receive this letter.

Your devoted friend,

Elizabeth

James Towne, Virginia

August 31, 1609

Dear Elizabeth,

Captain Tucker and Father have been working to build shelters for the families. Captain Tucker tells Mistress Pierce and Jane that if anyone can survive a hurricane, it is Captain Pierce. We still have had no word about the *Sea Venture.*

Our two blacksmiths work night and day making nails for building homes. The newcomers must build as many homes as possible inside the fort before winter. We will likely have several families or more in each home. I hope we are with Captain and Mistress Pierce and little Jane. I am quite fond of them.

For now, we are in a lean-to made of small trees and mats woven of reeds from the marsh. Mother and I weave the mats and my fingers are cut all over from the effort. We soak the reeds in water until they are soft and then weave them back and forth until we have a strong, tight mat. Father says our work will keep the rain from soaking us and he keeps us in good spirits as we weave. Temperance is not at all interested in weaving mats. I do not think she is ready for this adventure at all.

Your friend,

Abigail

James Towne, Virginia

September 2, 1609

Dear Elizabeth,

I have heard word that one of the supply ships will return to England next week. I will try to write as much as possible so my bundle of letters can reach you soon. I know you are very curious about my life here. Mother wants me to try to write to you after our day's chores are finished and before the sun is entirely gone. This is because there is so much work to be done.

We have all but given up hope that the *Sea Venture* will be saved. It has been six weeks now and no one has heard any word of the grand ship. All are feared dead. Mistress Pierce is very brave around Jane. At night, when Jane is asleep, I hear Mistress Pierce crying. Mother cares for her and comforts her. Poor Jane. I cannot imagine what it would be like without Father.

The so-called leaders of the colony continue to disagree. In my opinion, they are all selfish. No one thinks about what is good for the settlers. Winter will soon be here. Father says we must do what we can to preserve food. It seems most of the leaders are more interested in finding gold than finding food for the colonists. Father and Mother speak in hushed tones about food. I know they are concerned. I have seen Mother squirreling away as much of her ration as she can preserve, but food spoils so easily in this heat. Mother and Mistress Pierce are trying to garden, but as Mistress Pierce told Mother, the seeds are poor and have been sown late. We are not very hopeful.

I am trying to be nice to Temperance. I know you think she will be a friend and companion here, but, Elizabeth, there is not an ounce of adventure in her soul. She whimpers and frets and is simply not pleasant to be around. I will try, for your sake, to be her friend, but oh, she is tiresome. She worked beside me in a small garden plot today. All she could talk about was the market in London where she used to select her fresh vegetables. Well, this certainly is *not* London. If we are to have vegetables at all, we must work to get them.

Your friend,

Abigail

James Towne, Virginia

September 4, 1609

Dear Elizabeth,

Horrible things are happening here. John Martin, who came over on the *Falcon,* and sixty men went up river to trade with the Indians. Messengers were sent to offer copper and hatchets. The Indians killed them all. Apparently, Martin and his men took vengeance on the Indians and a deadly battle began. Many have died—both English and Indian.

Do you remember meeting Henry Spelman on the London dock? He came over on the ship with us and is twelve years old—the same age as you and me. Captain John Smith offered him in a trade for a Powhatan village! This village is filled with dry houses for lodging and land ready to plant. As part of the bargain, John Smith gave them Henry! Apparently, this is a way to show goodwill. We leave an English boy with the Indians, and they give us an Indian boy to live among us. It is all too strange for me. But think how strange it must be for poor Henry!

On his way back, Captain John Smith was terribly burned from an explosion. A spark ignited his gunpowder in a pouch at his waist. It is rumored he will return with the ships to

England. Then who will govern? And what about poor Henry if Captain Smith is not there to retrieve him!

The ship that takes Captain Smith back to England will also carry my letters to you. I have tied them in a bundle. I miss you dearly, Elizabeth. Tell your father that the state of things here in Virginia is not good at all, and beg him to do all in his power to convince the Company to send us supplies. The colony was not at all prepared for us and now we number nearly 500 souls. If only the *Sea Venture* had not been lost. Father tells me I must not be discouraged and that trying times are turning times. I do not know what he means. This new world is not at all what was described to us in London.

I suppose your summer was full of gala parties in the country. How very far away that all seems now. Please write to me soon. I will await your bundle of letters with great expectation.

Your friend,

Abigail

James Towne, Virginia

October 28, 1609

Dear Elizabeth,

I have nothing but bad news to give you. So many dreadful things are happening so fast. As soon as Captain Smith was injured, George Percy took over as president. He is very concerned about the shortage of food for the colonists. He told Father that the winters can be very cold here.

James Towne has other problems. President Percy sent Mr. Ratcliffe and fifty soldiers to negotiate with Chief Powhatan for corn. At first it seemed that the negotiations were going well. Chief Powhatan traded bread and venison for copper and blue glass beads. He even offered lodging for the men. The next day, our men collected the grain at the Indian storehouses. When Mr. Ratcliffe noticed that the Indians were using their hands to push up the bottom of the woven baskets to measure the grain and cheat us of the full measure, he was outraged. Words were exchanged and tempers flared. Then Chief Powhatan came out of a lodge with Henry Spelman! Henry must have been so very frightened. He had been traded once from the English to the Powhatans. What would happen now? Was he to be killed because of these angry Englishmen?

Mr. Ratcliffe ended the trading, and with the corn they already had, headed for their ship, the *Discovery.* Then they were ambushed! The Indians killed them one by one. They tried to capture the ship as well. Only sixteen of the traders returned to the ship, and Henry Spelman was not with them.

I spoke with Father about all of this. I am terribly afraid of the Indians. Though he was reluctant to tell me, Father explained that the English were not free of fault. They had killed many Indian women and children out of vengeance and spite. I was horrified to learn this. Father would not tell me more, but said that often things are not what they seem.

I will think about this.

Your friend,

Abigail

James Towne, Virginia

November 16, 1609

Dear Elizabeth,

More troubles. Captain Francis West and his crew of forty men sailed up river in the *Swallow* to trade with the Indians near the Potomac. They were friendly Indians, but Captain West killed many of them and burned their villages. Then on the way back, with their ship loaded with corn for James Towne, they stopped at Point Comfort. There they stole the *Swallow* and sailed for England. This is a terrible blow to the colony. We need the ship and the corn. Elizabeth, that's not all. They sailed without giving me a chance to send you my letters.

President Percy ordered Master Potts to take an inventory of how much food there is for the colony. It does not look good, Elizabeth. I heard Father tell Mother there is only half a can of corn meal a day for each person in the colony for three months. That is not nearly enough to get us through the winter.

Mother continues to work with Mistress Pierce digging for roots and berries that can be dried for the winter. She tries to stay in good spirits, but I can tell she is worried.

I do have a bit of good news. We are sharing a home with Mistress Pierce and Jane. Captain Tucker made sure of it.

He and Father are good friends now after having built so many homes together these last few months. Father says that although he knew Captain Tucker in London, it is here under the Virginia sun that their friendship has been sealed.

Mother enjoys the companionship of Mistress Pierce, who knows more about gardening than anyone else here. Mistress Pierce often clucks her tongue wishing that she had been here in the spring when it was planting season. She brought with her a number of boxes of seeds from her garden in England. She hopes the seawater that washed into the *Blessing* did not destroy the life in those seeds. If they are all right, she tells Mother, then we will have cabbages, turnips, onions, and carrots by this time next year. Right now all we have is a bit of meal made from these horrible root vegetables. Mother tells me this is what the Indians eat.

Your friend,

Abigail

London, England

December 3, 1609

Dearest Abigail,

I was so thrilled to receive your package of letters from the Captain of the *Blessing*. I will read them slowly and carefully. Thank you for making sure the letters were on the ship.

Father also brought me news of the injury Captain Smith received. The Company is greatly distressed, as the leaders they had chosen to govern the colony were all lost on the *Sea Venture*. Thomas Gates was to serve as the Governor of Virginia until Lord De La Warr could get here. Now Father says the Company wants to send Lord De La Warr to the colony as quickly as possible with supplies and additional men.

Mother is so pleased you and your parents survived the journey, as we have had news of many who did not. John wants to know about the horses and how they fare now.

You remain constantly in my prayers, and I remain

Your devoted friend,

Elizabeth

James Towne, Virginia

Christmas Day, 1609

Dear Elizabeth,

I can almost smell the goose cooking and taste the rich plum pudding. You are most certainly eating wondrous foods in the warmth of your country home. We had a paste of meal and water that Mother baked and then tried to make festive with a myrtle leaf perkily sticking out of the bread. Father continues to try to keep up our spirits. He read from the Bible of the wondrous birth of our Lord, and he reminded us that God still does miracles today. We need a miracle, Elizabeth, or we will all die. Four more dear souls died this very day. One was but a young child. This does not seem at all like Christmas.

For Mother, I will try to remain happy, but I am very worried about her. She seems so very frail.

Your friend,

Abigail

James Towne, Virginia

January 13, 1610

Dear Elizabeth,

You would have been proud of me today. I visited Temperance. She is so ill, Elizabeth. She didn't prattle on as she usually does. I told her I was bringing her a surprise. I brought her a linen handkerchief that survived the hurricane. I had worked her initials in thread pulled from the hem of Mother's brightest dress. She barely smiled when I gave her the present. Temperance lifted her hand in a gesture of thanks, but she was too weak to say much more.

Her eyes were very red, and I could see that she had been crying for a long time. I surprised myself, Elizabeth, by taking her in my arms to let her sob. I know how she feels.

This is a very scary time. Many people die each day. There is no more food. We are eating rats, snakes, acorns, and roots. There are those who have run out from the fort in desperation looking for food, only to be killed by the Indians. We are prisoners inside this fort—prisoners of our own hunger.

The old-timers tell of a young Indian princess called Pocahontas who used to visit and was kind to them. But no one has seen her for a long time. I wish she would help us get food.

Hunger does strange things to people. At first your stomach twists and turns in such pain. Then it becomes quiet—almost too quiet. Today a man ate his shoes. Another man ate his dog.

We began as 500 souls, but we are becoming fewer and fewer. The dead are buried at night so the Indians will not know how few of us are left. Many are near death. Mother is confined to bed now. She is too weak to get up. I have made her a soup of some sticks, a few acorns, and some leaves. I have to hold her head up so she can sip the soup. Father does not say much. He and Captain Tucker speak in hushed tones.

I am very frightened, Elizabeth. I know I should depend on God now more than ever, but if anything were to happen to my dear parents, I don't know what I would do.

We have heard word that Lord De La Warr will be coming soon. Supplies are desperately needed here. I don't know when you will get this letter. I trust that by the time you can read through the entire bundle, there will be a happy ending. I miss reading with you, Elizabeth. It seems so long ago that we read stories of life-threatening adventures and maidens rescued by heroes. Now I am living that adventure. I just need a hero.

Your very frightened friend,

Abigail

James Towne, Virginia

January 19, 1610

Dear Elizabeth,

Mother is much weaker. She can no longer sit up even for my pretend soup. Her skin is clammy, and her face is flushed. Mistress Pierce attends to her. She wrings out cloths of cool water to put on her fevered brow. I stand by so helpless.

I decided I had to do something to help Mother. I will not be able to bear it if she does not get better. So, long after nightfall, I found a hole in the palisade wall. It was a hole just the right size for me to slip through. Just as I had one foot and one shoulder through the wall, I felt a strong hand on my other shoulder. It was Captain Tucker on night guard duty. He has the awful duty of rationing out the remaining food supplies. He must do so even though mothers with starving children are clinging to him begging for more than their day's share. I turned and looked into his eyes. They were as warm as his hand was forceful.

"Where do you think you are going, young lady?" he said sternly.

"I must find my Mother some food. I can bear it no longer. She is so ill. If she does not get some food soon, she will die."

Captain Tucker pulled me back through the wall. "Abigail, your father is a good man. What do you think it would do to him if he lost you as well as his wife? I have something to show you."

I walked with him to the other side of the fort where he knocked the snow off a tarp covering a large lump. It was the beginnings of a small ship!

"Now you mustn't tell anyone. I have been working on this at night in secret."

"Captain Tucker! This is a large boat. Could it be big enough for . . ."

"Trading?" answered Captain Tucker. "I think so. Now, you must not tell a soul as I do not want anyone taking off in this boat before I have a chance to take it up river to trade for corn with the friendlier Indians. I still have some more work to do on it. Can you keep my secret?"

I nodded, and then, Elizabeth, Captain Tucker reached in his pocket and gave me seven kernels of corn. "For your mother, Abigail. And for you—to hope again."

I ran home with tears in my eyes. I am so happy. Soon we may have corn!

Your hopeful friend,

Abigail

James Towne, Virginia

February 16, 1610

Dear Elizabeth,

When I went home, Mother slowly chewed each kernel of Captain Tucker's corn. She wanted it to last and last. The next day, she was able to sit up again to take some of my pretend soup. She even laughed with me and said, "Let's pretend this is duck soup. Hmmm. So hot and delicious." It was so good to hear her laugh.

But now, Father paces the floor and checks on Mother every few minutes. She has taken a turn for the worse. It is so cold and Mother is skin and bones now. She cannot stay warm. There doesn't seem to be much we can do. Many people die each day. Others are weak from starvation and illness. I have been praying so hard for Mother. Why is she getting worse? Why doesn't God hear my prayers?

Father reads his Bible for long stretches of time. He seems greatly troubled. I have heard him talk very quietly with Captain Tucker outside the house. I strained to hear what they were saying, but all I could hear was "there's got to be a way" and "I have to do something."

Your friend,

Abigail

James Towne, Virginia

February 17, 1610

Dear Elizabeth,

    I am so frightened. Father and Captain Tucker left
during the night and they have not returned. I think they
had been talking about it for weeks. Mistress Pierce just hugs
me all day as we sit together and watch poor Mother.
Mistress Pierce told me that my father could not stand it any
longer. He felt so helpless, watching his blessed wife waste
away day after day and not being able to do anything about
it. I told her I knew that feeling too and almost told her
about the night I tried to leave the fort. I know exactly how
Father is feeling. I know with his lion's heart, he would do
anything he could to protect Mother and me. I hope Father
is just going to forage in the woods and not to try to trade
with the Indians. Word has it that Chief Powhatan has
instructed all his tribes not to trade with the English and to
kill them if they have the opportunity. Oh, Elizabeth, I am
trying to trust God in this.

Your friend,

Abigail

London, England

February 22, 1610

Dear Abigail,

I have not heard from you in such a long time. There have been no ships going to or coming from Virginia. Lord De La Warr was supposed to take the next supply to the colony, but he has been ill and the trip has been delayed until now. Lord De La Warr leaves for the colony and then the ships will return with news of you. I am praying for you, my dear friend. As I cannot know how you are doing yet, I will pray for you to stay strong and courageous.

Today the entire Virginia Company gathered at Temple Church. The members of the Council of Virginia were all there to commission Lord De La Warr as governor of the colony. Many of the shareholders, including Papa, attended this occasion of prayer and inspiration for the new colonists who will leave tomorrow. Reverend Crashaw preached a mighty sermon. He reminded Lord De La Warr and all the colonists what the purpose of these adventures really is.

He told all of us that we have a duty in four things: countenance, person, purse, and prayer. I, for one, will do my duty to God to pray for Lord De La Warr, as I know he is going to help my dearest friend.

Then Reverend Crashaw spoke to Lord De La Warr and said, "Thou art a General of Englishmen—nay, a General of Christian men. Therefore, principally look to religion. You go to commend it to the heathen. Then practice it yourself. Make the name of Christ be honorable, not hateful, unto them."

Remember when we attended church together. It was when you listened to Reverend Crashaw that your family decided to become adventurers too. Your father spoke with Papa and was greatly encouraged about being a part of the new colony. As I watched you listening to Reverend Crashaw, I wondered, dear Abigail, what was going on in your heart. Your eyes were glistening with tears. Were you afraid? Were you anxious? Were you feeling the tug in your heart that the Lord wanted you to trust him in this new adventure too?

Do not stop trusting him now. Know that he is your heavenly Father and he will not forget you.

I cannot wait until Lord De La Warr gets to Virginia and sends the supply ships back. I will await your next bundle of letters.

I have been diligent to pray for you every day. May the Lord keep you safe and bring me news of you soon. I am giving this letter and my others to Master Morgan, who is sailing tomorrow with Lord De La Warr on the *Starr.*

Your friend,

Elizabeth

James Towne, Virginia

February 23, 1610

Dear Elizabeth,

Captain Tucker returned last night with Father on his shoulders. He had been pierced by Indian arrows and had lost a great deal of blood. Captain Tucker carried him to his lodge, because we did not want Mother to know. Captain Tucker and Mistress Pierce attended to Father's wounds. When Father called out for me, Mistress Pierce brought me close to him. He grabbed my hand and said, "Do not lose faith. God will look after you whatever happens. Trust him with all your heart, and he will not forsake you." Then he died.

Temperance came when we buried Father. After the burial she hugged me and said I should come to her home where I could cry for Father. My tears would be too much for Mother. Elizabeth, it was Father who always kept our family strong. He is the one who encouraged us when we were afraid. Oh, Elizabeth, what if Mother dies too? Oh what will I do if I have neither father nor mother! I cannot bear the thought.

In deep agony,

Abigail

James Towne, Virginia

March 1, 1610

Dear Elizabeth,

Mother is still ill, and she still does not know about Father. Captain Tucker and Mistress Pierce explained to me that the shock would be too much for her. We must give her every reason to live. Mistress Pierce suggested I sit with her and talk with her as if nothing were wrong. It is so strange to do this, but I will do it for Father. He would want me to do everything possible to help Mother live.

With deep sadness,

Abigail

London, England

March 1, 1610

Dear Abigail,

Today Lord De La Warr and nearly 150 men with additional supplies left London. Since the ship carrying Captain John Smith arrived months ago, there has been no other ship going to or from Virginia. I pray you and your parents are well. I cannot stand waiting for word. At least now I know someone of great stature and commitment to the colony has left with ships of food. I cannot forget what you said in your letters written months ago about how little food there was in the colony and how ill-prepared the colony was to receive all the new adventurers. Captain Smith's reports to the Virginia Company stockholders only confirmed how desperate the situation is. Oh, dear Abigail, I am so hopeful now that I know Lord De La Warr has set sail. I will pray faithfully each day that he reaches you in time. Soon you will have my letters.

With great hope,

Elizabeth

James Towne, Virginia

March 3, 1610

Dear Elizabeth,

Last night, we were all asleep when I heard Mother stirring. I leapt up from the floor and came quickly to her side. She moved slightly and motioned for me to lie down beside her. I held her and sang to her the song she had sung to me all these years:

My little one, my precious one, do you know God loves you?
My little one, my precious one, do you know he cares?
He always is with you—in the dawn and in the night.
He will never leave you, nor forsake you,
He will guide you to his light.

I stroked her hair and thought of all she has done for me in my life. There was no greater sacrifice than the one she has made for me during this horrible, horrible winter. Before we ran out of food, Mother would share her daily ration with me. I could see that she was cutting back on her portion to give me more. I protested strongly, but Mother would hear nothing of it. Each day, she was giving up some of her food so I could live. What is my life without hers though?

I continued to stroke her hair and sing to her. Then as the morning sun was rising, she slipped away to heaven. Mistress Pierce had been up all night as well, but said nothing to me. She knew this time with Mother—these last few moments—was to be all mine.

We buried Mother today, and I returned, an orphan, to our home in James Towne.

Your friend,

Abigail

London, England

April 19, 1610

Dear Abigail,

We learned that Lord De La Warr took a shorter course. He should be in Virginia sooner than expected.

I have been unable to do much since I received your bundle of letters. Whether I am reading, going to a party, sewing, or taking lessons in stitchery, I think of you, dear friend. Mother urges me to continue my lessons on the lute, but how can I when it was always you who practiced with me? I miss you and I know I will feel so much better once I know Lord De La Warr has arrived, and you are well.

At least I will soon hear from you. The ships are due back for other supplies, and there are other supply ships scheduled to leave London soon. The *God Speed* leaves from London next month and I will have another bundle of letters on the ship. I am also concerned about your clothing, so Mother and I are putting together a bundle of clothing for you. Mother wants to add a few treats as well, such as soap and candles and seeds from her garden.

Your hopeful friend,

Elizabeth

James Towne, Virginia

May 4, 1610

Dear Elizabeth,

I could not write to you after Mother died. The grief has been too much to bear. Whenever I tried to write to you, dear Elizabeth, my tears spilled onto the paper and smeared the ink. I would crumple up the letter and throw it against the wall. I was so angry, and yet I could not compose myself enough to share with you, my dearest friend, what I have been feeling. I will try again now, for I long for your company again. You have been faithful to write to me, I am sure, and I know you must have been frightened for us when you heard the news about Captain Smith and the sad state of the colony. This bundle of letters is piling up. Yet we have had no word from England or any hope of assistance since September.

My heart is burdened with grief. I spend many days crying with Mistress Pierce just holding me until my eyes are too tired to cry any more. Mistress Pierce told me I will continue to live at their house. Captain Tucker spoke with President Percy who has agreed to this, at least until passage to England can be arranged. Mistress Pierce has been very kind to me, but I have made up my mind. I am an English girl, and I will return to England. I will forget this place ever existed—if it can continue to exist at all.

The settlement is greatly troubled, Elizabeth. There are no supplies, no food, and no relief from London. The rats scavenged what few provisions we had left. We are imprisoned inside the fort. We cannot fish. We cannot hunt. We cannot grow food. Oh, for a handful of corn! Those hateful Powhatans will not trade with us. They simply wait for anyone who dares to come outside the fort, and then they kill them—just as they did Father. One day the Powhatans promised to trade for corn. Several of our men agreed to leave the safety of the fort to make the trade. They were all killed. Those Powhatans are tricksters! They promised corn only to kill the men sent to get it.

It is horrible inside the fort. Elizabeth, you would not have been able to abide it. Men ate dogs, rats, snakes, anything they could to stay alive. Do not tell poor John, but there is not a horse left alive now.

Before the winter, we numbered 500, but with the warmth of spring, only sixty of us are left. I am so thin and very heartsick after losing Father and Mother, but I refuse to die. I will see you again. I hunger to return to London. Soon, very soon, I will be able to come home. Temperance is also going home. Just as soon as the next ship arrives, if we can make it that long. We will come home together. I promise I will never, ever say another bad thing about Temperance.

One needs more than a spirit of adventure to make it here in this dreaded place. I miss you so much, Elizabeth, but soon, I will be with you again. That thought alone will keep me alive. I will think of England and the River Thames and reading poetry with you. I do not know what I will do as an orphan or where I will live. I just want to be on English soil again and to be with you. Perhaps Uncle Samuel will take me in at Warwickshire.

Your very English friend,
who is no more an adventurer,

Abigail

James Towne, Virginia

May 16, 1610

Dear Elizabeth,

Mistress Pierce is so thin. She has been as true to me as Mother. She continues to halve her portion of acorns or berries with Jane and me. She is very careful to protect from decay the stores of dried nuts and berries that she and Mother had gathered, and although we nibble on just an acorn a day, it sustains us still. Few, though, are left alive. Captain Tucker, our cape merchant, stopped by twice in the last few weeks to bring us a special ration. He told me his shallop boat is now finished, and he is ready to take it out to trade. President Percy, however, has determined that he will take the shallop and go to Point Comfort to see how those there fared during this awful time. All are more hopeful now, as Captain Tucker's shallop will be large enough for us to escape if aid does not come soon.

Your soon-to-be-across-
the-Atlantic friend,

Abigail

James Towne, Virginia

May 18, 1610

Dear Elizabeth,

I am so furious I could scream. President Percy and Captain Tucker returned from Fort Algernon at Point Comfort. A few soldiers were sent there months ago. I had feared for their lives and had wondered if President Percy would find anyone alive. I wasted my concern. Captain Tucker reported that almost all were fit as a fiddle and enjoying the abundance of crabs and oysters found along the shore. President Percy was furious too. I overheard him tell Captain Tucker that the crabs these men fed to their hogs would have been a great relief to us and saved many lives. They also kept two of the small ships, the *Virginia* and the *Discovery,* for fishing in the bay. Just think what Captain Tucker could have done with those ships if they had been at James Towne! Selfish, selfish men.

President Percy decided he would take half of us (there are only sixty left now) to the Point for food and when that half recover, the other half will go to the Point. If all else fails, we will abandon this dreadful colony. President Percy speaks well when he said that another town or fort might be erected or built, but men's lives, once lost, can never be recovered.

Captain Tucker wants Mistress Pierce, Jane, and me to go in the first half, but we protested. There are others in much worse straits than we are. We can wait another few weeks.

If the truth be known, I don't know what I would do to those men if I saw them—fat and happy, while almost all of those in the colony starved to death. They were so selfish and unwilling to share the food or the ships. If Father could have had that ship for one day, I know he could have found fish for Mother and me. I am so angry, Elizabeth. These are people with no souls who only think of themselves and fatten their bellies while those nearby starved.

With men like this, this colony cannot survive.

Your furious friend,

Abigail

James Towne, Virginia

May 23, 1610

Dear Elizabeth,

I will stay up all night and use three candles if I have to in order to write you this amazing news. The *Sea Venture* landed today! Well, not really the *Sea Venture* itself. It was shipwrecked in Bermuda. All were not lost!

Early in the morning, a sentry on the fort spotted two small ships drifting to James Towne on calm waters. Captain Tucker told Mistress Pierce, Jane, and me to stay inside the house until it was known whether they were friend or foe. Imagine our surprise when President Percy stepped off the first ship. The ships landed at Fort Algernon at Point Comfort two days ago to the surprise of President Percy, who had taken some of the most ill among us to the fort. He came with them to James Towne. One by one, nearly 150 adventurers walked down the planks from the two ships. The new governor, Sir Thomas Gates, and Admiral Somers, Vice Admiral Newport, and all the others. All save two who boarded the *Sea Venture* in London a year ago are safe! It is a miraculous story.

They arrived in two small ships called the *Patience* and the *Deliverance.* Perfect names for these ships, don't you agree? The thirty of us left in the fort ran out to meet them, but they looked at us in horror. I think we looked like skeletons in ragged clothing. That was when I noticed. Every one of the *Sea Venture* passengers looked healthy and well fed.

Captain Tucker helped the women and children down from the ship, and we all gathered around to greet them. Then the men began to walk down the plank from the ship. Mistress Pierce gasped. Oh, Elizabeth, what joy! There was Captain Pierce, as hale and hearty as ever. He swept little Jane up in his arms and Mistress Pierce kept patting his arm as if she could not believe he was really standing there next to her.

The last man to leave the ship was Admiral Somers. He saw me standing alone and walked over to me. Admiral Somers asked after Father, and when I shook my head and looked away, he put his strong hand on my shoulder. After a moment, I turned back to him and said simply, "Mother too." He gave a deep sigh, and in one sweeping glance, looked around the fort and sighed deeply again. Sir George Yeardley spoke briefly with Temperance and her mother.

I know your parents will want to know about the Rolfes. Mistress Rolfe survived the awful voyage and gave birth to a daughter soon after landing on Bermuda. Reverend Bucke, their dear friend, christened the baby girl and named her Bermuda. She died several days later.

The church bell rang out and everyone gathered for prayer. Reverend Bucke prayed for us all and wept openly at the devastation of our colony. He asked God to grant wisdom to our new governor, Sir Thomas Gates, and show us the way. I silently prayed the way would be straight back to England. After the service, Master William Strachey read the governor's commission and President Percy surrendered his commission to Governor Gates. Now we will see what he decides will become of us.

After the service, Governor Gates began to assess the situation here at James Towne. He seemed rather shocked. When I saw what he was looking at, I began to see why. Much of the palisade wall is in disrepair. The gates to the musket holes hung by a hinge. Of course, we had used the abandoned houses of those who had died for firewood. I am sure President Percy was filling him in on the situation with the terrible Indians as well. I can tell there will be many meetings to decide our fate, but today is for celebration, especially for the Pierces.

Captain Pierce, Mistress Pierce, and little Jane walked arm in arm toward our home. I decided to stay with Temperance so that they could have some time together. I shared with Temperance that although I was very glad to see their family reunited, it made me miss Mother and Father all the more. I will not think about that today, however, for today is a day of great tales of adventure and miracles.

We gathered the *Sea Venture* colonists together to hear their tale. No one cared at that moment that there was still too little food for the sixty of us and now the additional 150 new colonists. We were hungry for tales of adventure.

Remember the hurricane that clipped all of the ships in the *Sea Venture*'s convoy? Well, the *Sea Venture* had the worst of it. Master William Strachey, long involved with the London theater, told the tale. The story he told today was better than any play you might see in London, dear Elizabeth. We all sat down on mats, and he leapt on a bench to tell the tale in a most dramatic fashion.

This is the story he told:

The clouds gathered thick upon the *Sea Venture* and the winds were singing and whistling most unusually. A darkness came upon us that beat the light from heaven, and it turned terribly black. Every captain on board said we were in trouble. Admiral Somers, an experienced seaman, knew we were in the midst of a hurricane. The *Sea Venture* took on water. From noon on Tuesday until Friday, the ship lurched from side to side as the winds blew us toward the dreaded Bermuda islands. Many a ship has wrecked upon the reefs near those islands, never to be heard from again. Admiral Somers was at the helm, never sleeping, never standing down, but ever aware of the dreadful coast of the Bermudas and what that could mean for the *Sea Venture.*

It did not just rain. Oh, no. It was as if a river was flooding the air. Not only was the ship taking on water from the skies but the winds pushed the sea water in billowing waves over the ship's deck and into her hull. The women and children stayed below deck even as the water was rising rapidly. There was a mighty leak that caused the ship to draw five feet of water. Even the most seasoned mariners were frightened. Every man was at work. They crept along the ribs of the ship searching every corner and listening in every place to hear the water run. They found many leaks and repaired them speedily. Despite this careful search, the leak that took in the greatest seas and caused our worst destruction could not be found. The crew worked nonstop with pumps and buckets to try to clear the water from the ship's hold. Biscuits and meat were floating everywhere.

Admiral Somers divided the men into three groups and told each man where to stand. Every man took the bucket or pump for one hour and then rested for the next. This way, we continued for three days and four nights.

One time, a huge wave covered the ship from stern to stem and almost filled the hold. The force was so violent that it tore the man from the helm, and ripped the whipstaff out of his hand. Although he was tossed violently from side to side, it was God's mercy that he was not broken in two. When he came up, bruised and battered, but with whipstaff in hand, unbroken, it was a cause of encouragement for all, and the passengers cheered.

Admiral Somers was ever a strong encourager. He cried out in a loud voice for one and all to keep bailing. Not one man failed to serve the others in the task before us. On Thursday night, Admiral Somers saw a little round light much like a faint star. He called the others to observe as the strange light, like firelight, stayed with us for the whole night. The Bermudas are said to be enchanted and filled with witches and devils. Some of the men thought this was a tempest of evil.

To stay afloat, sailors threw over much luggage and trunks and chests. Much of the food and barrels of oil and cider were heaved over the side to try to lighten the ship. By Friday, there was great despair. After having bailed and pumped thousands of gallons of water, the poor adventurers on the *Sea Venture* were giving up hope. They were ready to commend their sinful souls to God and commit the ship to the mercy of the sea.

Reverend Bucke knelt on the deck and began to pray, "O most glorious and gracious Lord God, who dwellest in heaven, but beholdest all things below: Look down, we beseech thee, and hear us, calling out of the depth of misery and out of the jaws of this death, which is ready now to swallow us up. Save, Lord, or else we perish. The living shall praise thee. Oh, send thy word of command to rebuke the raging winds and the roaring sea that we, being delivered from this distress, may live to serve thee and glorify thy name all the days of our lives. Hear, Lord, and save us, for the infinite merits of our blessed Savior, thy Son, our Lord Jesus Christ."

No sooner had he said his Amen, than Admiral Somers cried out, "Land!" Everyone cheered and thanked God. Admiral Somers and his crew worked to bring the ship in, and about a half mile out from the Bermuda Islands, the ship crashed first into one rock and then another and became wedged between the two. Upright! Oh this was not a loss but a joy, for it was low tide. All the men, women, and children safely made it to shore. They sank down on the sand with shouts of joy and many tears. All were so relieved to have made it to land safe and sound that they did not care if a Bermuda witch was there to meet them! Ah, but it was not Devil's Island, as has been thought for so long. There the refugees fed on fish, fruits, berries, and many wild black hogs, which was a tremendous blessing since all of their provisions had been lost in the storm. (Elizabeth, that is the only part of the story that was hard to hear, as I am still very hungry.)

Master Strachey said, "It pleased our merciful God to make even this hideous and hated place both the place of our safety and the means of our deliverance." (Hmm, Elizabeth, I'd like God to make this hideous and hated place of James Towne my place of safety and deliverance, but nonetheless, soon I will be back in England where I will eat to my heart's content.)

Master Strachey continued:

For all these months, we lived there in ease. The climate was delightful for most of the ten months, and the food was plentiful. The men cut down cedar trees of much strong wood and with cables, oak planks, and some pitch and tar— salvaged from the *Sea Venture*—we began to rebuild. We were very hopeful.

On Christmas Eve, we had a wedding between Admiral Somers' cook, Master Thomas Powell, and Elizabeth Persons. On February 11, 1610, we christened the baby daughter of Mr. and Mrs. Rolfe and named her Bermuda. Sweet Bermuda died shortly after that. Captain Newport and I were there to witness the christening. Twice on Sunday, Reverend Bucke preached, and we gathered every morning and evening at the ringing of the ship's bell for public prayer.

Admiral Somers launched his ship in April to see if she was seaworthy. She sailed well, and Admiral Somers named her the *Patience.* The other ship was named the *Deliverance.* Now it was just a matter of waiting for the best winds to head to Virginia. Once the ships were ready, Governor Gates set up a cross in Admiral Somers' garden. It was made of timber from our ruined ship. Next to the cross were these words:

"In memory of our great deliverance, both from a mighty storm and leak, we have set up this memorial to the honor of God. It is the spoil of an English ship of three hundred ton called the *Sea Venture,* bound with seven ships more, from which the storm divided us, to Virginia."

With the strong winds, it was less than a week's journey from Bermuda to here. Just think, Elizabeth, they were that close to us all the time.

Oh, I am so excited, I do not know if I will sleep tonight. We had more to eat tonight. I had something called conch that is a kind of fish from Bermuda.

This is the first day I have been happy in so long. I imagine I will tell you this in person before you receive this letter, dear Elizabeth.

Your friend,

Abigail

James Towne, Virginia

May 29, 1610

Dear Elizabeth,

Governor Gates called us all together today. He told us that he has enough food on board the two ships to feed us all for two weeks using a ration of two fish cakes per day. Of course, to those of us who have eaten acorns and dried roots every day for months, this sounds like a grand feast. If the men find nothing in the countryside in two weeks, he will make ready and transport us all to England. A great cheer went up on both sides. Of course, all of us here would leave tomorrow, and I think our friends from the *Sea Venture* now know that this is not the colony they were promised.

We who have been here this last year know that it will be impossible for them to find food in this short time. Powhatan's tribes will not help the English. The days of Princess Pocahontas bringing baskets of food are fairy tales now.

Your not-so-hungry friend,

Abigail

James Towne, Virginia

June 6, 1610

Dear Elizabeth,

   The James River usually has plenty of sturgeon at this time of year, but there is not a fish to be found. The men hauled their net twenty times through the river, but there was nothing. Governor Gates sent the longboat down to Point Comfort to fish, but after one week, they caught only a few fish. It is a divine proclamation that we are to go home! I am secretly thrilled with each report of failure to find food. There is only one course left to take—abandon this god-forsaken colony and go home to England!

   Recently Governor Gates met with Admiral Somers, Captain Newport, Captain Percy, and others. They have decided to abandon the fort and set sail with all of the colonists in the four ships that are left—the *Discovery*, the *Virginia*, the *Deliverance*, and the *Patience*. We will head directly to Newfoundland to meet up with other English ships bound for England. I cannot wait to sail out of this dreadful place.

Your very-ready-to-come-home friend,

Abigail

Mulberry Island, Virginia

June 8, 1610

Dear Elizabeth,

I could not write to you yesterday. We are all so very busy. Governor Gates ordered his men to strip the houses of all possessions, pack them in barrels, and load them on the ships. I kept Father's Bible, Mother's wedding ring, and my paper, ink, and quill pen, along with my bundle of letters to you. Soon I will deliver these letters to you in person. We languish at Mulberry Island, anchored here for the day. As soon as the tide turns, we will set sail.

The men worked all morning to load the ship. At noon, all boarded the ship to the beating of the drum. Governor Gates and Captain George Yeardley stayed behind on shore. Captain Pierce told me that it was because of a plot to burn the fort. They can burn it to the ground for all I care. Finally, Captain Yeardley gave a farewell salute to the abandoned fort, and we lifted anchor. I have never been so happy. Good-bye, James Towne. Good-bye, America.

Your friend,

Abigail

James Towne, Virginia

June 11, 1610

Dear Elizabeth,

My fortunes have changed again! Dear Elizabeth, this adventure continues to take such twists and turns. I know you will think me mad, but I believe God would have me stay in America. Let me tell you what has happened.

We were anchored at Mulberry Island waiting for the tide to turn when suddenly the lookout on the *Deliverance* cried out. He had sighted a boat coming up river toward us. It was Lord De La Warr himself with 150 men and enough provisions for a year. He ordered us all back to the fort. Some were happy, but others were quite sad. The colonists have been through so much during this starvation time; most just want to go home.

When we stepped back on the shore of the fort, Lord De La Warr immediately knelt down and thanked God that he had arrived in time to save James Towne. He then strode with great authority directly to the church, where he requested that Reverend Bucke deliver a sermon. And what a sermon it was! We all listened with rapt attention, for truly the hand of the Lord was in our salvation from certain death and the ruin of the colony.

Reverend Bucke spoke of the direct intervention of God. He reminded us that if God had not sent Sir Thomas Gates from the Bermudas, we would have been out of food within a week and left to die a terrible death. If God had not directed Sir Gates to preserve the fort as we were leaving several days ago, we would not have had a fort to come back to now. If we had abandoned the fort earlier, then surely the Indians would have burned it to the ground. If we had not been held for a few hours by the whims of the tide at Mulberry Island, we would have missed the amazing deliverance God planned for us in Lord De La Warr's arrival. If God had not directed Lord De La Warr to bring with him enough food for 400 people for a year, surely we would not be staying now. This was the arm of God that had done all these things. How could we fail to trust him?

I marveled at Reverend Bucke's words and found my heart stirred again as it had been when I was in England and listened to Reverend Crashaw's sermon. Perhaps God *is* in control of my life here—at James Towne—in America. Perhaps God has a reason, which I cannot see yet, for allowing me to survive the horrible time of starvation. Perhaps God has something for me here.

After the sermon, Lord De La Warr's commission as governor for life was read to us, and then he told us of the new rules we must live under. They are tough rules, but Father always said that it would require a strong disciplinarian to make something of these weak-willed men.

Captain Pierce told me he spoke with Lord De La Warr about arranging for me and Temperance to return to England when the first of these three supply ships returns. But suddenly I feel strange inside. I am not sure I want to go now. I do not feel the fear I once did about this land. Instead, I feel strangely excited—like a new adventure is about to begin. I will keep these thoughts to myself and ponder them to see if they be of the Lord or of my own adventurous heart. At least I know this much, dear Elizabeth, my spirit of adventure has returned!

Your friend,

Abigail

James Towne, Virginia

June 16, 1610

Dearest Elizabeth,

I have just received the barrel you and your dear mother packed for me and sent in Lord De La Warr's fleet of ships.

Thank you for the warm jacket. I will not need it right now, but next winter, it will be of great use to me. Mistress Pierce is very excited about the seeds you sent. The best of all, though, was your bundle of precious letters. I cannot wait to read them. I miss you so much, Elizabeth.

Dear Admiral Somers has gone again. He volunteered to return to Bermuda to obtain provisions there. He plans to bring back wild hogs, fish, and some birds. We saw him off today on the *Patience*. Governor Gates is going to return to London next month on the *Blessing* to make his report to the Virginia Company. I will send you my letters then.

Your friend,

Abigail

London, England

September 18, 1610

Dear Abigail,

You were so good to put the packet of letters on the *Blessing.* Sir Thomas Gates, your governor, and Captain Newport brought them back to England and gave them to Papa. After reading them, however, I am so surprised you were not on the ship with them. I cannot bear to read about the horrible things you have been through this last year.

Oh, my precious, special friend. You have been so long now in the New World. I am deeply troubled over all the reports so widely known here in London about the many troubles of the Virginia Company's James Towne settlement. How horrid are the tales of starvation and Indian attacks. Abigail, you must have been horribly frightened during that awful time. Had not Lord De La Warr arrived when he did, you might have died.

Abigail, I was so grieved to hear the news of the deaths of your parents. I will miss them as much as if they were my own family for they always treated me so.

You must feel terribly alone. Why did you choose not to return to London where Mother, Papa, and I could take care of you? I know you are a determined, adventurous girl, but

Abigail, it is so dangerous there with the Indians and all. What has possessed you to stay? Papa told me you refused to return to England with this ship. I do not understand. You seemed so ready to return to England in your last letter.

Please, dear Abigail, write to me and let me know how you are. Papa tells me there will be many supply ships to the colony this year. That means you and I will be able to send our letters more frequently. Do not forget, dear friend, that if you want to return to England, Papa has told Governor Gates that you are welcome to return to us anytime. I will pray faithfully for you, dear friend. I miss your company sorely.

With a grief-stricken heart, I remain,

Faithfully your friend,

Elizabeth

James Towne, Virginia

October 5, 1610

Dear Elizabeth,

There is so little time to write now. We have been rebuilding James Towne and everyone has been hard at work. By summer's end, we repaired the palisades, constructed a new church, and built many houses. These homes are much more durable lodgings. You would think we are turning into Indians. We are building the new houses long, like the Indians do, and covering them on the outside with bark. We have also been making mats from the marsh reeds, just like the Indians, to cover the inside of the houses. Even the youngest children help with the weaving.

Elizabeth, you should see our church now. It rivals any cathedral in England. It is sixty feet long and thirty feet wide and made entirely out of cedar—the church, the pews, the chancel, and the pulpit. There is a communion table made of black walnut. The church has fair, broad windows to let in the light, and two bells hang in the end of the church to call worshipers to the services. Lord De La Warr requires that fresh flowers be placed in the church every day. That is my job and I like my job a great deal. I take a few extra minutes when I put the flowers in the vase on the communion table to tell God what I am thinking.

Mistress Pierce and I have been working in the garden most of the day. We do not say it to one another, but I know we are both thinking that we will never again have a winter like the last one. The seeds your mother sent to us are wonderful. They sprouted well, and we are growing wonderful vegetables. We will have a feast later this year. We planted your mother's impractical, but very beautiful, flower seeds. Mistress Pierce agreed to let me have a small corner of our garden for the flowers. She realizes that the flowers will not only encourage everyone in the church but also fill my soul with happiness. I only wish Mother were here to garden with me. She always loved to grow flowers in our garden back in England. Thank your sweet parents for me.

I am afraid I have some bad news for your mother. Her friend Mistress Rolfe died last month from a terrible fever. The summer here is such a sickly time, and many came down with fevers. John Rolfe is very sad, but he spends much of his time with Reverend Bucke in prayer and mutual encouragement. Master Rolfe has lost both his baby daughter and his wife now in just a few months' time. I have spoken to him several times, and he seems quite agreeable.

Your friend,

Abigail

James Towne, Virginia

October 8, 1610

Dear Elizabeth,

I want to tell you about our church services. We have two church services every weekday and two sermons every Sunday—one in the morning and one in the afternoon. There are strict laws about attending church. Lord De La Warr thinks laws will give some of the lazy, willful men a better understanding of the values needed to build a community here in Virginia. When the bells ring, we all stop what we are doing to pray.

On Sunday the bells ring. Lord De La Warr marches to church with a guard of fifty men in bright red cloaks. Some walk beside him, some walk behind him. They march up from his ship where he lives. Behind this party are the members of the Council, the other officers, and then all the gentlemen. Inside the church, Lord De La Warr sits in a green velvet chair with a scarlet velvet cushion spread out before him on a bench for him to kneel. When the service is over, he leaves in the same manner. It is quite a sight to see.

Now, think of us next Sunday when you are at St. Paul's!

Your friend,

Abigail

James Towne, Virginia

October 10, 1610

Dear Elizabeth,

There is a supply ship leaving the colony tomorrow for England. I am rushing to get this letter to you. I am sorry I have not written much. Those of us who made it through the starvation time work harder than anyone else. We know the importance of sufficient food and warm shelter.

Temperance returns on this ship. She has begged me to go with her, but I am not ready. I told her there is more to this adventure than I have yet experienced. Temperance looked at me with surprise and said, "I would think losing your parents and nearly starving to death would be adventure enough." She is probably right, but something is keeping me here. I don't know what it is, but I sense my time in America is not yet over. I bear her no hard feelings for returning. In fact, as you predicted, I have rather come to like her. There is not much companionship for a girl my age, and I will miss her.

Please let me know if you hear anything of Sir George Somers, the beloved admiral of our ill-fated fleet. No more selfless a man is there anywhere. He is the one who saved all those passengers on the *Sea Venture* by keeping up men's spirits as they bailed and pumped water from the ship for four days. He is the one who skillfully guided the *Sea Venture* between the two rocks so that all made it to land safely. He is the one who worked night and day with the carpenters there on Bermuda to build two seaworthy vessels in which to come to us. And now, he is the one who volunteered to return to Bermuda for additional supplies. No one has heard anything from him, and he should have been back by now.

Tell your parents that the Pierces have been very kind to me, and I am well. I know they are worried about my safety here, but Captain Pierce is very brave and keeps a watchful eye on Mistress Pierce, Jane, and me. He often uses his breaks from building houses to come by the garden to make sure we are faring well.

Your friend,

Abigail

London, England

October 18, 1610

Dearest Abigail,

I just returned from the most glorious party at Middleton Hall in Warwickshire. It was a wondrous affair. I wish you had been here with me. I have so much to tell you, and I will not forget a single detail.

Carriages arrived all day and evening bringing guests from London and the countryside. Sir Wentworth startled everyone by arriving from Oxfordshire in the finest coach pulled by six horses festooned with plumes. All the men were enthralled with the coach, one of the first of its kind, designed by Mr. Bridges. The tassels were silk. The curtains were the finest leather. The Wentworth coat of arms was gilded on the side of the new coach. I heard Papa tell Mother the coach cost 20 pounds! Imagine that! As much as three of the horses!

Let me tell you about some of the people I saw there, Abigail. Many at the party are stockholders in the Virginia Company and there was much talk of James Towne. I will tell you more about that in a moment. First, I must share the most wondrous news conveyed to me at the party. Sir Henry Wriothesley, Earl of Southampton, and Sir William

Herbert, Earl of Pembroke, were both in attendance. Papa told me that they are the patrons of William Shakespeare. I wanted so to meet them and Papa introduced me to them. They told Papa that Master Shakespeare is working on a new play about the dreaded voyage of the *Sea Venture* that wrecked in Bermuda two summers ago.

Apparently, from what the Earl of Pembroke was saying, Master Shakespeare is fascinated with the accounts of what happened during the horrible storm when the survivors reported a strange glow that appeared at the mast of the ship. You should ask Master Rolfe when you see him about the glow. What was it like? Sir William says that Shakespeare will make a character out of the mist and the glow, as only he can. I wish Papa would let me attend. He says it is not proper for a child of my upbringing to attend the theater, but he might make an exception in this case. After all, it is about your grand adventure. I think it would be wonderful to attend one of Master Shakespeare's plays.

Many of the royal knighthood, who are stockholders in the Company, were at the party. Even Sir Oliver Cromwell. There was much talk about the status of life in Virginia. The Company is debating whether to send more settlers to James Towne. There is some concern among the gentlemen that the return on their investment may be meager indeed. The hope of much to be made from the discovery and the return of gold is dwindling.

Many wonder if the James Towne experiment was folly. Some believe that the venture will result in many conversions of the savages to Christianity. Others believe that the savages are devil-inspired to quench the flame of truth.

Papa says we must be patient. He believes the Lord is doing a great thing in the New World, and great things often come with great sacrifice. I think of the sacrifices you have made in order to go with your parents to the New World, Abigail.

The manor house was incredibly lovely. Fall flowers were in full bloom in the gardens. And the Cliftons were such gracious hosts. Papa tells me they are quite hospitable and charitably entertain all, from the King to the poorest beggar. Middleton Hall was certainly fit for a king at this party.

The day began with the men going hunting. The Middleton estate has deer, rabbits, pheasants, partridges, and pigeons, some of which we ate for dinner that evening. Papa was with the group that went hawking.

The ladies gathered in the sitting room to share news. When Mother felt the news had turned to gossip, she suggested I might want to see the library. Of course, I was quite interested in the news, but obeyed her nonetheless. And I am so glad I did. Oh, Abigail, the books there! I counted them— more than 300. I could have stayed with them forever. Only when Mother interrupted me did I realize I had been reading for more than two hours. I wish I could go to university at Oxford or Cambridge. I do not understand why formal schooling should be only for the men.

When Mother urged me outside, I took a walk in the gardens. There were pear trees and apple trees and cherry trees. Orchards as far as the eye could see. Papa says Sir Clifton has at least forty men who tend the gardens. But it is Lady Clifton who should be praised. She showed Mother and me what has been filling her time this last year. The accomplishments included building a dove house, planting one of the cherry orchards, and designing the garden in which I found myself. She confessed to me that she had designed the chapel by relying on a copy of *Palladio's First Book of Architecture*, which she found in her husband's library. Surely if a gentlewoman such as she can build such a lovely building, a gentlewoman such as I can go to Oxford!

Alas, until I am allowed to attend the fine school, I will have to make do with talking to the gentlemen who by the fortune of birth are able to study. Many young men from Oxford College were in attendance at the party. Such learned men and so handsome. Abigail, Robert Buxton was there. You remember him, don't you? He has grown quite tall and handsome since you left. He left London for Oxford last year. He is not the young boy who used to pester us so horribly when we were younger. To the contrary, he is quite remarkably pleasant. In fact, I danced with him most of the evening. You would have truly enjoyed him, Abigail. What is left of his bothersome youth is only his energy and curiosity. He has become a well-mannered, winsome gentleman, worthy of further conversation, I dare say! I hope to see him again before he returns to Oxford. His delightful brother, Adam, was in attendance as well—so perfect for you! He inquired about your well-being.

I thought of you all evening. Do you not miss the excitement, Abigail? Would you not rather be here with me attending galas and having such wondrous experiences? How can the New World compare to the Old? I simply do not understand why you do not return to me posthaste, dearest friend. I will continue to pray for this miracle. I miss you terribly.

Your devoted friend,

Elizabeth

London, England

November 20, 1610

Dear Abigail,

Father came home from the Council meeting where Governor Gates and Captain Newport reported such horrible events in James Towne. Lord De La Warr sent a letter to the Council stating in no uncertain terms that they must immediately send more supplies and doctors and medicine. He said that half the remaining members of the colony have died.

Father said the Council spoke many hours with Governor Gates and Captain Newport. They debated whether to try for a new contribution of funds or simply abandon the entire Virginia venture. They asked Governor Gates if what had been reported was true and asked him to give his own report of the conditions in Virginia.

Sir Gates said that Virginia was one of the goodliest countries under the sun, blessed with a healthful climate. Sir Gates also predicted that oranges and lemons would grow there, as a lonely orange tree transplanted to James Towne had survived the winter. He also noted that there were an amazing number of white mulberry trees—the kind needed for the production of silk. If silkworms were introduced to the colony, it's possible the product would be of better quality than that from Italy.

Father says the Company is much encouraged and interested in Bermuda as well. They have decided to raise more money for the venture. Another fleet of colonists may be arriving in just a few months! Perhaps, you are truly on the verge of another adventure.

Mother admires your hard work and has been hinting that I would do well to take up some gardening myself. I would rather read, however, *in the garden,* than weed the garden. I am to take up French lessons soon, and Mother plans for a tutor to teach me geography. I will ask to learn everything I can about the New World.

I envy my brother John, who is able to go to school. I wish they would allow girls to attend. For now, I will learn as much as I can from books. I am glad John shares his day's lessons with me. I am eager to learn and do not understand why only the boys have this advantage.

Your friend,

Elizabeth

James Towne, Virginia

November 23, 1610

Dear Elizabeth,

You will be amazed when I tell you what happened this week. Henry Spelman returned! What a tale he had to tell about his adventures. Henry Spelman was sent to America to become a young man of valor. Apparently, he got into some trouble in London and his family thought learning to survive in Virginia would be good for him. When the *Unity* landed and Henry walked down the plank to solid ground, I am sure he never imagined he would be taken by President John Smith and traded for some Indian land as a gesture of good will. He was terrified once he learned of the attack on Captain Ratcliffe as he was the one who was told by Powhatan to tell the English that they could trade with him. When that trading session became a massacre, Henry was afraid for his life.

Later, he met Chief Pasptanze, chief of the Patawomekes, who came to visit Chief Powhatan. The chief of the Patawomekes showed kindness to the three English boys who were residing there—Thomas Savage, a boy known only as Samuel, and Henry. The boys decided they wanted to leave with Chief Pasptanze. After they had gone half a mile, Thomas had a change of heart and went back to live with Chief Powhatan. He ran off and told Chief Powhatan what was happening. Chief Powhatan sent his men after them. They struck Samuel with an ax, and he was killed. Henry was terrified and ran faster. Just when he thought he could run no farther, guess who helped him? Pocahontas. That's right. She had been sent to the Patawonekes by her father, Chief Powhatan, as an agent for the tax he collected from each tribe. Pocahontas and Chief Pasptanze helped Henry to escape, and he has been living with the Patawomekes far up the river from James Towne ever since.

Had not Captain Argall been trading in the Patawomekes' territory, Henry would be there to this day. Captain Argall first asked for the English boy he had heard was there to help in the trading. Chief Pasptanze permitted Henry Spelman to serve as an interpreter during the trading, but before the trading was over, Captain Argall traded a large amount of copper for Henry himself!

Tonight we stayed up late listening to Henry's tales. He lived with the friendly Patawomekes for more than a year. During that time, he got to know Pocahontas very well. He says he likes her very much, and she is very smart. She learned some English from John Smith, but Henry says he taught her even more. Henry is quite good at the Powhatan language, but the words are quite funny. Did you know they say *cohattayough* for summer? Tell John to try this on his schoolmates: *Wingapo!* (It means "hello.")

Many were rejoicing in James Towne when they learned that the Indian princess who had done so much good for the colony in its early days was still willing to help an English boy. Many of the old-timers in the colony who remember her visits as a young girl had always wondered what happened to her. It has been several years since they last saw her.

I, for one, think it is fine if she just stays with the Pata-womekes. The Indians, with or without this princess, are not friends of ours.

We are thankful for Captain Argall's successful trading visit. Now we have a large cargo of corn, some venison, and some furs—and Henry!

Your friend,

Abigail

London, England

December 1, 1610

Dear Abigail,

Tonight I accompanied Mother and Papa to a wonderful ball. We danced the whole night long. There were some wonderful new young gentlemen who caught my eye. However, I spent most of the night with Temperance Flowerdew.

Temperance is glad she is back in England. She has shared about the awful time of starvation. Abigail, you spared me many of the details that Temperance has now told me. What a horrid, horrid time.

Temperance is puzzled about why you decided to stay. I tried to tell her you have an adventurous soul, but she said, "That wasn't an adventure; that was a death sentence."

I cannot imagine being in that dreary land, swatting bugs, fingernails filthy from digging for food in a garden. You must come home. We both miss you.

Your friend,

Elizabeth

James Towne, Virginia

December 5, 1610

Dear Elizabeth,

This year we are preparing for Christmas. It will be nothing like the last year, except that I will read from Father's Bible. Captain and Mistress Pierce, Jane, and I are planning a grand celebration with turnips and cabbages from our garden, oysters, and dried berries.

We have had bad news about Admiral Somers. He died in Bermuda after filling the ship with many supplies for us. His last words were begging the men with him to take the *Patience* straightaway to Virginia. Those selfish men took the ship, laden with food, for themselves.

Your friend,

Abigail

London, England

January 13, 1611

Dear Abigail,

I have wonderful news for you, my stubborn friend who will not come home to me. The Company has raised sufficient funds and will not be abandoning the colony. The Company will soon send three ships under the command of Sir Thomas Dale. Several hundred able-bodied persons will go with him. Papa says a wonderful parish minister with whom he has become acquainted is going to accompany Sir Dale to Virginia. Papa says you should be sure to make his acquaintance when he arrives. His name is Alexander Whitaker. He told Papa that when he has spoken with Reverend Crashaw and sought the Lord in his quiet moments, he finds his heart strangely turned toward Virginia. The reports of the Indians move him to want to come to share the good news of Jesus Christ with them. He is strong and unafraid. I think he is an adventurer like you. Mother does not understand why he would give up such a lovely parish in the north of England for the difficulties of the New World. I must warn you. Father has spoken to Reverend Whitaker about your need for instruction in the catechism. Father is particularly concerned about you as an orphan there in Virginia with no father or mother to give you proper instruction in the ways of the English and in the Christian faith. I suspect your free-spirited days may be coming to a close, dear friend. I can see you now, bringing flowers to the church and having special times of instruction in the ordinances of the church—rather than your wonderful times of prayer with God.

Father is concerned that the young people are not being well instructed in Virginia, and he keeps a watchful eye on my education as well. If only he would let me learn more than French, music training, and church doctrine. I want to study so much more, but Father says that the things I am interested in are reserved for my brother, John. John has not one whit of interest in book learning. He would much rather be outdoors training in archery or horsemanship.

John was pleased to hear that more horses are being sent to Virginia. He told me to tell you to please not eat them.

Your frustrated friend who is
not quite as adventurous as you,

Elizabeth

James Towne, Virginia

March 28, 1611

Dear Elizabeth,

Lord De La Warr has set sail to find relief for his illness. We do not know if, or when, he will return. We had a wonderful visit with Captain Adams of the *Blessing* this month. Do you remember that he was the dear captain who led us through the hurricane on the way to Virginia? He still commands our dear ship, which is none the worse for the storm. He brought us news of the soon coming of Sir Thomas Dale, who will be the marshal of the colony. We will soon be under military law. Oh dear, Elizabeth, you know how I am about rules. The punishments are dire, so I must obey.

Best of all, Captain Adams brought me another barrel from your family. Thank you so much for the ink and paper and set of fresh quills. You do not need to worry about sending quills in the future as geese and turkey are plentiful here. I am able to make my own pens. Mistress Pierce thanks your mother again for the abundant supply of seeds, which came at exactly the right time for planting. I see you have sent me the *Book of Common Prayer* to study along with your letter about Reverend Whitaker. I simply have no time for such study as we are in the garden from sunup to sundown. Mistress Pierce is determined to have the largest and most productive garden of all. We each must have our own plot now, so that the lazy ones will not eat unless they plant crops.

Tell brother John that I promise not to eat the horses, but the pig . . . well that's another story.

Your friend,

Abigail

James Towne, Virginia

May 10, 1611

Dear Elizabeth,

Marshal Dale arrived today with several hundred new colonists. It is always a fun time when we meet the new people. I love to watch their faces as they realize what they were told about wonderful James Towne is not exactly true. It takes several days for the look of shock to wear off their faces, especially the mothers. After what you now know about Virginia, could you imagine what it would be like to leave your comfortable life in London and your country home? French lessons would be over in an instant. No lute lessons here. Just roll up your sleeves and start to work.

More children are beginning to come to the colony. I am glad as I do miss Temperance. You were right to say that I would need a friend my age. So far, the children are much younger than we are. There are no girls our age. Jane is sweet, but she is so much younger than we are. I am soon to be fourteen—almost a grown woman.

The three supply ships brought many animals. The fort is overrun right now with chickens, pigs, and cattle. It is a good thing we had already built a stable and a shelter for the cattle this last year.

Sir Thomas Dale greeted John Rolfe. Apparently they knew each other before. He introduced Master Rolfe to Reverend Whitaker. Reverend Whitaker seems nice enough. Captain Pierce tells me he is 26 and that he left a very prosperous parish in northern England to administer the holy sacraments of the Church of England here in Virginia. Reverend Bucke, Master Rolfe, and Reverend Whitaker spoke together for quite some time. I am sure Reverend Bucke is glad to have another minister here to help.

Of course, it is almost summer, and I suppose we will again lose many to the fevers that plague our colony. It seems the newcomers are especially vulnerable. Mistress Pierce calls it the "seasoning time." She says if you can make it through the first summer here, you are likely to be strong enough to stay.

Well, I think I will stay busy and out of sight. I have no time for lessons now in church doctrine or anything else for that matter. Frankly, Elizabeth, I do not miss it. Why you have such a hunger to study books is something I cannot understand. You should have been born a boy, dear friend, for the only books you will be allowed to read are fairy tales.

Your friend,

Abigail

James Towne, Virginia

May 12, 1611

Dear Elizabeth,

One of the first things Marshal Dale did was to post the *Laws Divine, Moral, and Martial* in James Towne. I read just a few of the new laws. Whew! We are going to have to watch our tongues, our manners, and our actions. The first time a man fails to attend church services without showing good cause, he forfeits his week's allowance of food; the second time, he is whipped; and the third time, he is to be shot or hanged! I suppose church attendance will be more regular now.

Marshal Dale took men from the fort here at James Towne to repair Fort Henry and Fort Charles, built by Lord De La Warr. The men left here are to cut as many trees as possible while he is away. Captain Pierce has heard rumors of a new settlement up the river.

I know the air is so unhealthy there in London during the summer. Will your family go to the country?

Your simple friend,

Abigail

London, England

June 1, 1611

Dearest Abigail,

Sir Thomas Gates is about to leave with nine ships, much provisions, more settlers, and many soldiers to help fight the Indians. I am beginning to feel better about your situation. Now you will have food and protection.

Father is encouraged as he sees that the Company has created new interest in the James Towne colony and many more good people are willing to risk going to America. Father knows several of those going with Sir Gates. He is bringing his wife and two daughters with him as well. I hope the girls will be good company for you.

I must hurry. Father is going to take this letter to the ship for me in a barrel of more surprises for you. We love you so much, Abigail. Take very good care of yourself.

Your friend,

Elizabeth

James Towne, Virginia

July 1, 1611

Dear Elizabeth,

The rumor is true. The Supreme Council in London has apparently approved Marshal Dale's plan. The fort will be at James Towne, but the settlements are to be elsewhere. He decided to make certain there are settlers up and down the James River so that the Indians can never throw us into disorder again like the time we were all held captive in one fort. He has taken a party of good men to sail up the James River in search of places to build new towns. Reverend Whitaker went with him. I think they are good friends.

Must go. I have much work to do in the garden.

Your friend,

Abigail

James Towne, Virginia

July 26, 1611

Dear Elizabeth,

It is official. Marshal Dale has set aside seven acres for the first settlement. It is located about fifty miles upstream from James Towne. Men are working very hard to cut down enough trees and make enough lumber for the new buildings. They are building a cattle shed, a stable, and a blacksmith's forge. Others are trying to produce bricks for chimneys. The storehouse is in need of repairs, and Captain Pierce and Captain Tucker are working to build a munitions house and powder magazine to store the weapons we will need to defend ourselves.

I am sorry my letters are so short, but we are very busy. With church services twice a day and my regular duties, I fall asleep quickly at night. I will write more soon—I promise.

Your friend,

Abigail

James Towne, Virginia

August 2, 1611

Dear Elizabeth,

Governor Gates arrived today with nine ships filled with supplies! Why there must be more than 100 cattle! I think I saw an ox as well, which should help with the plowing of the fields. So many soldiers! Governor Gates went to the Tower of London while he was in England. He has brought so much old armor that was just sitting on the shelves there in the Tower that now we have no idea where we will put it. I don't think the Indian arrows will pierce our men now!

Oh, Elizabeth, I have such sad news. Lady Gates, the wife of the Governor, died on the trip over. Mistress Pierce told me that Governor Gates will return his two daughters to London. I think I would have liked his girls too. I still yearn for company of a girl my age, but one who also has a spirit of adventure. Yet, I am so busy here that I probably would not have time to be a good friend. Why, look how hard it is to get a few moments to write to you!

Your friend,

Abigail

James Towne, Virginia

September 3, 1611

Dear Elizabeth,

I am staying up late. With the light of this candle, I will write to you until the candle burns out. It is said that some of the ships are returning to London soon.

You asked in your letters why I do not return to England. I know it must seem strange that I would want to stay here now, especially after all those letters I sent to you last year. I know our lives are very different. It's just that I can't shake the feeling that I am supposed to be here. There has to be some reason why I did not die in the awful starving time. I feel deep in my soul that I am needed here. For what, I do not know. Perhaps it is not yet time to know.

Today, as I slipped inside the church with fresh flowers, I knelt before the altar and prayed. I had Father's Bible with me and opened it to Jeremiah 29:11. Listen to what it says: "'For I know the thoughts that I think toward you,' saith the Lord, 'thoughts of peace, and not of evil, to give you an expected end.'"

Yes, I nearly died. My precious parents did die. I am an orphan in a strange land. But I know in my heart that I have a heavenly Father who has made me a promise. There are plans for a future and a hope—right here—right where I am. If I leave now, I may never know what those plans were. I simply must find out.

Your dear family has been so kind to me. There is not a ship that arrives here without some word from you, dearest Elizabeth, or a present from your dear parents. They have sent me clothing, seeds, and writing paper and ink. And, of course, your dear Father, worrying about my education, has sent me the *Book of Common Prayer* and a hornbook to practice my penmanship. Please do not tell him I have no time to read and am simply too tired at night to hold a book.

You, your mother, and your father have all written to me separately to tell me that your family would take me in if I returned to England. I know this is true. Ever since my dear parents died, your family has cared for me. I even had a note from John that said I could live with you if I didn't eat his horse. Your family is so special to me. Only a higher call would keep me from rushing home to live with you.

I hope you will understand. It is not something I can easily explain. It's just that when I have my quiet moments in the church arranging the flowers for the day's services, I know deep in my heart that I am to remain here—at least for now.

Your friendship will never ever be far from my mind or heart. Remember when we were saying good-bye—two years ago now? We were just twelve then. It has been such a long time since I have seen your delightful smile. I can scarcely remember your image. It is a good thing we traced each other's hands before I boarded the ship. What a grand idea that was. I have noticed though that my hand is quite a bit bigger than the hand you left with me. How you must have changed since we were last together. We may be growing up and our bodies are changing, but our hearts will forever remain the same—dedicated to each other.

Forever your dearest friend,

Abigail

P.S. I don't mind if you are friends with Temperance. I would have been jealous when we were younger, but she is a good friend and our link to one another. Though she is in London, she is well acquainted with life here and can tell you all about it. I, on the other hand, am such a poor letter writer. I promise to improve.

P.P.S. I must rush. The ship is due to leave soon. Guess who is returning with the ship? Master William Strachey, the great dramatic story teller of the *Sea Venture.* You simply must meet him. You and Temperance should ask your father to invite him to visit and tell the story again.

James Towne, Virginia

September 27, 1611

Dear Elizabeth,

There is much excitement here. Marshal Dale took 350 men and ships full of timber posts and planks up the James River to the settlement he intends to fortify. It will be called the Citie of Henricus after Prince Henry. You should have seen the men march off in full armor. Captain Pierce went with them. Now he is back for more supplies. He told us that in only ten days, the men had strongly impaled seven acres of ground for the town. It will be at least ten times the size of James Towne.

The men are building blockhouses and watch towers at the corners of the town. A separate storehouse will be built so that food, tools, rope, canvas, trading goods, and clothing can all be kept under the control of the Cape Merchant there. Captain Pierce could not stay long. Marshal Dale is making quick work of this business of building a new town. Captain Pierce had to return quickly with pitch, timber, and nails and hinges from our blacksmiths.

The women and girls here have been making rush mats for the lodgings. My fingers are bloody from the work. Yet there is a spirit of excitement in the air. The soldiers have fended off the Indians and there is a sense that this new palisades high on a bluff over the James River may survive any attack. Marshal Dale has quite an eye for defense. Those many years he was a solider in the Dutch lands are surely not going to waste here.

I can't help wondering what Henricus is like. Captain Pierce says there is a long view and fertile valleys nearby. He thinks the air is healthier than here at James Towne. I wonder who will go to live at Henricus? Will Captain Pierce move our family there? I rather like it here at James Towne, but these new tales pinch my soul with adventure!

Your friend,

Abigail

London, England

November 1, 1611

Dear Abigail,

Today Papa and Mother are traveling to the palace at Whitehall and the court of King James, who invited my parents to the performance tonight! The King's Men, William Shakespeare's company, will perform his latest play, *The Tempest*. Many of the Company council will be there as this is not your usual Shakespearean play. I do so wish I could see it. Papa tells me that from what he has heard from Shakespeare's patron, Sir Henry Wriothesley, it is based on the shipwreck of the *Sea Venture*.

Mother was dressed so beautifully in her gold brocade jacket and blue satin skirt. I helped Mother fix her hair, but I really wanted to be going myself.

Your friend,

Elizabeth

London, England

November 6, 1611

Dear Abigail,

I just read your long letter, and I want you to know that I may not be able to really understand what is going on in your life there in James Towne, but I have felt the tug of the Lord on my heart many times. I know that it is something you cannot deny. I will support you in this great adventure of yours.

Master Strachey has many reports to make to the Council here. I will ask Papa to invite him for dinner and Temperance too. I am sure she would enjoy seeing him again.

I prayed a special prayer for you, asking the Lord to send you a special friend, one with whom you can share your adventure every day.

John wants me to thank you for the package you sent to him. He wants to know if the arrow was ever in anyone's back. Yuk. I'm sorry to even ask you, but I promised John I would.

Your devoted friend,

Elizabeth

James Towne, Virginia

November 19, 1611

Dear Elizabeth,

Captain Pierce told us that the building is nearly complete at Henricus. Marshal Dale and the men have been hard at work. They are also building four additional forts: Fort Charity, Mount Malady, Fort Elizabeth, and Fort Patience. Mount Malady will be our first official hospital. The builders are completing a parsonage for Reverend Whitaker just a short distance from Mount Malady and across the river from the Citie of Henricus. Captain Pierce says the land set aside for Reverend Whitaker's church (they call it a glebe farm) will be well protected right there in the middle of all those forts.

Reverend Whitaker spends a lot of time with Reverend Bucke here at James Towne. Reverend Bucke has only been here since May. He was in Bermuda helping the colonists for nearly a year before that. I guess Reverend Whitaker wants to learn how to shepherd us sheep here at James Towne.

Last week I placed the flowers in the church. As I was having my special time alone with God, I was surprised to realize that Reverend Whitaker had been standing there, probably for quite some time. Reverend Whitaker said he was sorry to startle me, but he had come in very quietly so as not to interrupt my prayer time. We spoke for a few moments.

I told him that Captain Pierce reported to us that the parsonage was coming along nicely. Reverend Whitaker said the parsonage is in Coxendale, which means "hope in faith," and that he is going to name it Rock Hall. I must have given him a funny look, because he laughed and said, "I see you think it is an odd name."

I said, "Well, it's just that Captain Pierce told me that the buildings there are made of timber piles and planks and wattle and daub, not rocks."

"Ah!" replied Reverend Whitaker. "I want to name it Rock Hall because of what that means to me. You see, Miss Abigail Matthews, there is a verse in the Bible that is special to me. I see you have a Bible. May I?"

I held Father's Bible close to my chest. No one else has touched that Bible since Father and Mother died. Reverend Whitaker didn't reach for it. He didn't ask for it again. It was as if he knew—and understood.

"Here it is. Let me read this to you, Abigail, from Matthew 16. Jesus is with his disciples, and they have seen him perform many miracles. He has healed the sick. He has walked on water. He has multiplied loaves of bread and fish for the crowd to eat.

"Now he is alone with his disciples and asks them who people say that he is. They give him lots of answers. Then he asks them personally, each of them, 'Whom do you say I am?' Abigail, do you remember who answered?"

I just shook my head. Reverend Whitaker continued, "It was Peter. Oh, how I like Peter. He is headstrong, opinionated, quick with answers and action. No one is going to count Peter out. Well, Peter says, 'Thou art the Christ, the Son of the Living God.'

"Abigail, you can almost hear the excitement in Jesus' voice as he says to Peter, 'Blessed art thou, Simon Bar-jona: for flesh and blood hath not revealed it unto thee, but my Father which is in heaven.' Can you imagine, Abigail? Jesus has been walking and living with these men for a while and finally, finally, one of them understands his mission, the reason God sent him to earth. He knows that this kind of special insight only comes from his Father, but oh, how it must have thrilled him to see a willing hearer of his Father's message. Do you know what happened next?"

I was as quiet as a church mouse. I wondered what in the world this had to do with naming his parsonage Rock Hall. He continued, "The most wondrous thing, Abigail. Jesus gave Simon, son of Jonah, a new name! He said, 'And I say also unto thee, that thou art Peter.' Abigail, a new name! Simon—impulsive, headstrong Simon, was given a new name, a name of Jesus' choosing. Simon would be Simon no more. No, now he would be Peter."

Elizabeth, I know my face must have shown how puzzled I was. What in the world did this have to do with Rock Hall?

Reverend Whitaker laughed. "I see I have confused you, Abigail. Let me tell you what happened next. Jesus said, 'Upon this rock I will build my church; and the gates of hell will not prevail against it. I will give unto thee the keys of the kingdom of heaven; and whatever thou shalt bind on earth shalt be bound in heaven: and whatever thou shalt loose on earth shall be loosed in heaven.'"

Elizabeth, now I was really confused. I didn't understand a word Reverend Whitaker was saying about binding and loosing on earth and in heaven. It didn't make a bit of sense to me, but I didn't want to hurt his feelings. After all, he is so excited about being a preacher. I pretended to look sufficiently enlightened and said, "Oh, I see, Jesus wanted to build his church on a rock and so do you."

Reverend Whitaker smiled. "Abigail, I know God sent me here to help others know who Jesus is." Then he paused, and added, "Especially the Indians."

Well, Elizabeth, that was that. I wasn't going to stand around and talk about my God being brought to the very people who killed my Father and starved my Mother. No, sir. I turned on my heels and ran out. I know it was rude, but I did not care. If Reverend Whitaker had been here last winter, he would never have said a thing like that.

He's a nice man who has a lot to learn about life in America.

Your opinionated, headstrong
friend who doesn't want a new name,

Abigail

James Towne, Virginia

November 30, 1611

Dear Elizabeth,

John must be wondering about the bow and arrow. I should have written him earlier to let him know that it is a real and true Indian bow. Captain Pierce found it and gave it to me to send to John. He thought he would enjoy it. Please let John know that the arrow is real, but it missed its mark, which was a squirrel, not a person. Captain Pierce told me that the bow is the right size for a boy John's age. It is made of locust wood and has deer sinew for the string of the bow. Tell John it is likely that an Indian boy made this bow himself using a shell to scrape the wood until it was the right size and shape.

Elizabeth, I have pressed some of the flowers from my garden that go in the church. I will send some of them to you on the next ship to London. I am also sending you a quill pen I made just for you. Now you can say you have a pen made from a turkey from Virginia. It will do my heart good to know you are using the pen I made for you when you write to me.

Master Rolfe hopes a ship arrives soon from the West Indies. He is expecting some special tobacco seeds that he hopes will grow here. He thinks the climate is exactly right for it. I showed him some tobacco that grows wild in this area—the Indians use it. But Master Rolfe told me it is bitter and would never sell in London.

I must close now. The sun goes down so early this time of year. At least as winter arrives, we are not worried. My stomach is filled with turkey, goose, wild pigeon, oysters, berries, vegetables, and corn. I do miss the wondrous delicacies of cakes and tarts though, dear Elizabeth. Hmmm, are you making gingerbread this Christmas? I must not think of sweets too often. But I do miss them, dear Elizabeth.

Your friend,

Abigail

James Towne, Virginia

February 3, 1612

Dear Elizabeth,

I did so miss you and your family at Christmas this year. Please give this enclosed note of thanks and appreciation to your father for his thoughtful Christmas gift to me—a King James Bible. How wonderful! I will keep it with Father's Geneva Bible. I tried to reassure your father that my training as a young Christian lady is going along quite well. I think he is still concerned though. It is true that my training has not gone as yours would there. Your training is formal—once a week catechism classes and special tutoring by your parish minister. Mine happens as I just live my life here. The church bell rings, and we all gather to pray and hear a good word from the Holy Scriptures given by either Reverend Bucke or Reverend Whitaker. They are both wonderful preachers. But I also see them every day, and we talk about spiritual things while I garden or sew while sitting on a bench outside, or while I walk with them to the river. A class is not needful. I rather enjoy our talks about God. Please tell your father that things are different here but still the same, and not to worry.

You cannot imagine the changes that are taking place. In four months, Marshal Dale and his men have built four forts and the new settlement, Henricus. Reverend Whitaker will leave after the snow melts to live at Rock Hall (you know the place where people with new names get to live). Reverend Whitaker means well, but he can't be serious about telling the Indians about Jesus. They won't believe it anyway. They are afraid of their god named Okee. He is mean, and they have to make sure they make sacrifices to him so he won't be angry with them and ruin their crops. Oh well, Reverend Whitaker will figure it out soon enough.

A number of the new adventurers who have arrived in the last year have asked me about Pocahontas. As if I would know! She is myth and legend from all I can tell. They heard she had rescued an English boy. You remember Henry Spelman, who ran away from Chief Powhatan and barely escaped with his life. Supposedly, if Pocahontas had not helped him escape, he would have died. I think it is a story made of pure imagination. Henry is known for his exaggerations anyway. He thinks he is something special because he knows both English and much of the Powhatan language after living among the Patawomekes for more than a year. He says he learned a great deal from Pocahontas, but I do not believe him.

If she is so caring about the English, then where was she during the starving time? Certainly she was no friend to the English during that winter! Old-timers speak about her in awe. They tell tales of when she would come carrying baskets loaded with food. She used to play with the boys at the James Towne fort and turn cartwheels in the street. I think she was just a show-off. Some say they would like to meet her. Not me. I don't care if she is a princess of Chief Powhatan. She can stay away forever.

I hope your father, bless his soul, is not still worried about my education as a young lady. Tell him Mistress Pierce is making sure I know my stitches. We sew many of the shirts for the soldiers who came over with Marshal Dale. He has had them working so hard that they rip through many shirts over a short period. The women and girls help with the mending and sewing.

I hope you told your father about my conversations with Reverend Whitaker so he can be assured my religious education is not lacking. I do think he worries about me too much. Have you had any success convincing your father to let you have a tutor for science? I know he thinks that is not a proper subject for girls. If you were here, you could work with Master Rolfe in his tobacco experiments!

Your friend,

Abigail

London, England

March 12, 1612

Dear Abigail,

Papa came home very excited tonight. The Virginia Company received its new charter today from King James. The King has extended the boundaries of Virginia to include Bermuda Island where the *Sea Venture* wrecked. Some here are calling the islands Somers Islands after that most selfless of all mariners, Admiral George Somers, who volunteered to go back to the island to secure food for the colony and there met his death. Papa also says that the King will now permit the colonists in Virginia to own private land. He thinks that will attract new settlers as well.

The Virginia Company stockholders are encouraged by the reports from Marshal Dale and Governor Gates. I had not wanted to tell you this before, but Papa had been concerned that many of the investors would no longer want to be a stockholder in the Virginia Company but would put their money behind the East India Company instead. Although we do get a good supply of timber, potash, sassafras, and pitch, many here were more interested in the more exotic goods that were coming from East India, such as tea, spices, silks, and indigo. Even Captain Newport resigned as admiral for the Virginia Company and is now providing his skills and services to the East India Company.

Some of those who had pledged money for the Virginia Company have never paid. Papa and some of the other stockholders have been devising plans to raise more money. He told me to tell you not to worry, for the King has granted the Virginia Company a right to a lottery. He expects that many funds will be raised soon for the colony.

Your friend,

Elizabeth

London, England

April 19, 1612

Dear Abigail,

If I hurry, I will be able to write this letter to you and gather it with my letter written a few weeks past to accompany Captain Argall on the *Treasurer.*

Papa also says to tell you he has placed a chest of special things just for you on the ship. He and mother love you dearly, and although he did not say, I think a special silk dress made by our tailor was included. There is also a beautiful embroidered robe for formal occasions. Papa told me that he included something terribly impractical for you. He told me he wanted to lavish a special present on you to demonstrate his and mother's high regard for you, dear Abigail. I miss you, dear friend. Would that we could be sitting in our garden together pretending to study our literature and yet sharing such wondrous secrets!

Your devoted friend,

Elizabeth

Rock Hall, Henricus, Virginia

July 26, 1612

Dear Elizabeth,

I received your good letters when Captain Argall and the *Treasurer* arrived from London last month. I apologize for not writing to you sooner, but my life has been turned upside down again! There have been so many changes.

As you know, your father was concerned about my instruction in godly things. He spoke with Governor Gates when he returned to London and told him that he wanted me to be instructed in catechism, the Bible, and the doctrines of the church. Governor Gates spoke with Marshal Dale, and it was decided. I had no say in it. Neither did Captain or Mistress Pierce. It was for the good of the colony that I have been sent to live at Rock Hall near Henricus. I am now miles and miles away from James Towne. I am here to help Reverend Whitaker with his church in the same way I helped Reverend Bucke with our church in James Towne. Mrs. Sizemore, who is Reverend Whitaker's housekeeper, has been assigned to help me become a proper English woman.

I miss the Pierces so much. Mistress Pierce understood when I stayed up late from time to time crying about my parents. I remember one night when I hurt so much inside my heart. I tried, Elizabeth. I tried so very hard to remember Mother's voice. I used to be able to hear it in my head, and then one day it was simply gone. I didn't want it to be gone. I wanted to remember her sound, her fragrance, her touch as she brushed my hair from my face when she kissed me good night. I wanted to say to her just once more, "Good night and good rest" and hear her say again, "I pray God that so it be with you. God be with you."

It was Mistress Pierce who understood. She let me sob in her arms until I had no strength. She listened to me as I told her about not being able to hear Mother's voice in my head anymore. She brushed my hair away from my face like Mother once did. And Jane was so good. She didn't mind my being in her family. Captain Pierce always said that he would care for me out of the respect he held for Father. I didn't want to leave. It was so hard and I was so angry that I couldn't even put it down on paper in a letter to you. Besides, I have so much copy work now my hand smarts from practicing my alphabet and copying passages from the Bible.

Please don't tell your father. I know he meant well, but I am so unhappy. I miss James Towne, the Pierces, my friends, and my garden.

Your lonely friend,

Abigail

Rock Hall

July 27, 1612

Dearest Elizabeth,

How thoughtless of me! I just poured out my troubles to you and did not even once thank you and your father for the gifts. I think your father needs to come over here and see how we live. The silk dress and robe are glorious, but I doubt I will have any occasion to wear them. Nonetheless, I will look at them and think of you and how beautiful you must look when you go to the ball and dance the night away.

You and your family are so dear to me and your father has always treated me like one of his own. I am most happy to be so loved by your parents (with the exception of this campaign to make Abigail Matthews into a proper English lady).

Reverend Whitaker wrote a long letter to the Virginia Company yesterday. He asked me to copy it for my hand-writing copy work so that he would have a copy of what he had said. It was rather like a Sunday sermon and took me a very long time to copy it, but it made me think.

Reverend Whitaker urged the stockholders to care about God's kingdom here in America and not be so concerned with making a profit from the colony in America. He urged each of them to be generous and to care more about others, especially the Indians and their need for God, than themselves. Now I am not sure I agree concerning the Indian part, but his letter made me realize some things about myself.

You think I am brave and full of faith to live this life here in Virginia. Well, I think you are wrong. After I copied what Reverend Whitaker was saying in his letter, I realized I am very selfish. I want everything to return to the way it was. I want to live with the Pierces. I want to live in James Towne. I want to be free and not have to learn so many proper English things (like proper handwriting and spelling). I want my own way. I guess that is just pure sin—wanting what I want when I want it. I have decided to try to listen carefully in my prayer time. Perhaps God is doing something here at Rock Hall, and I need to stop focusing on myself and my frustrations and see what he is up to.

Isn't that what a life of faith is all about, anyway?

Your not-so-angry friend,

Abigail

London, England

October 16, 1612

Dear Abigail,

There is such excitement in the city. Frederick V, the future king of Bohemia, arrived in London today. Soon he will wed Princess Elizabeth. That will be a wondrous event with so many festivities. I know I will go to many parties this winter, and for that, I am glad. I do so like to dance and wear new dresses. I wish you were here to go with me. Temperance sends you her best as well. Did you know she writes Captain George Yeardley from time to time? He is a soldier there with Marshal Dale. I think he is sweet on Temperance, but Temperance thinks not.

Your friend,

Elizabeth

Rock Hall

October 22, 1612

Dear Elizabeth,

Marshal Dale has encouraged others to consider moving to special lands along the river. Marshal Dale and his men have been making them safe places for the people to live and there are now five forts. There is talk about many people in James Towne moving up the river. Maybe the Pierces will move near here, and I can see them more often. Besides, today Reverend Whitaker preached on all things working together for the good of those who love God. If the Bible really means all things, then it includes my living here at Rock Hall.

To be fair, Elizabeth, Reverend Whitaker is wonderful to me. He knows I was angry about having to leave the Pierce family and my friends. He has told me that flowers are needful in his church as well and has given me a much larger garden than I had in James Towne. He depends on the storehouse for his grain, so he told me I did not have to plant much corn at all. Instead, he said I could plant as many flowers as my heart desired. If your kind mother would send me some seeds on the next ship, I will make good use of them in the spring.

It is beautiful here, Elizabeth. The air is so much cleaner and fresher than near the marsh in James Towne. Even the bugs did not seem to bite so much this summer. It is peaceful here at Rock Hall with plenty of land to roam. I suppose that it also helps some that Rock Hall is up the river from James Towne. My memories of Mother and Father are stronger in James Towne. Reverend Whitaker says God is giving me a new start here, and that he will take care of me. I just wish he had taken care of Mother and Father. I do miss them so.

Captain Argall stopped by on the *Treasurer*. Marshal Dale sent him to trade for corn with the Indians. If he gets much corn, he may come back to fill our storehouses as well. I asked him when he is going to London next as I want to have my letters ready for you. He said he will be busy trading and exploring for the next few months. It may be a while before my letters can find their way to you. I wish we could see each other. I miss you so much, dear friend.

Your friend,

Abigail

Rock Hall

November 5, 1612

My dearest Elizabeth,

How I miss you, sweet Elizabeth! I will have to take comfort in these letters until we can be together again. I miss you more about this time as we used to celebrate our birthdays together. Mine on October 18 and yours on November 1. Just think—we are now young ladies of fifteen years of age. I imagine that a young lady of fifteen in England has a life much different from that of a young lady of fifteen in a certain Virginia colony. Why, I imagine that your shoes are polished and bright, while mine are worn thin and must last until the next ship. Please ask your father to send me a pair of sturdy shoes in the next consignment! No more silk dresses!

I will tell you about Reverend Whitaker in this letter. Rock Hall is my home now and Reverend Whitaker, the tender of my soul. Mrs. Sizemore, Reverend Whitaker's housekeeper, and other ladies in the church are most kind. They mean well, Elizabeth, but they can't replace my mother. They are certainly trying hard to tame the wildness out of me and bring me up proper. I would still much rather dig in the garden than practice my lettering or stitching.

I miss Mother. She seemed to understand my need to run free and explore and have adventures. I am well suited for this journey and this grand adventure. I do not miss London much at all. I find I am in the most trouble when I have been stitching for oh, too long and all that is in me yearns to run to my garden or climb a tree for the long view. I know I am fifteen now and must abide by the rules of womanhood, but the skirts are too constricting, and perhaps the etiquette is as well.

Reverend Whitaker has undertaken to school me in all Truth. I have scripture lessons with him daily. He is quite concerned for my impetuous spirit, especially when it comes to my still blazing anger toward the Indians . . . and at times, toward God. I cannot help it, dear Elizabeth. It does not make sense to me at all. I am to trust God to take care of me, the orphan, but was it not he who has forsaken me? He forsook my mother and my father—that is certain. Now it is just me, alone, remaining.

Reverend Whitaker tells me I must not let this bitter root fester. I pretend I am all done with bitter roots and have scuttled them into the compost heap. I pretend I am brave, but in the night and in my letters, I tell you what is true. I miss my parents sorely.

Good night, sweet Elizabeth. I will write to you again soon. Ever your admiring friend, I remain

Faithfully yours,

Abigail

Rock Hall

December 4, 1612

Dearest Elizabeth,

You will never believe what happened. In the middle of Reverend Whitaker's sermon, a songbird flew in and could not be persuaded to leave. The men ran around flapping their hats at the bird. And the women were all atwitter themselves. In my head I was cheering on the bird.

Reverend Whitaker had just read from the Holy Scriptures that we are to consider the birds of the field, how they neither toil nor labor. When the bird flew in, it was much better than any picture in a book. However, I am afraid I am the only one who saw it that way.

Andrew Martin missed church for the second time. Reverend Whitaker has told me that the law requires a public whipping of twice-offenders. When I asked about Martin's fate, Reverend Whitaker said he was not certain the law was the best way to bring the reluctant ones back into the fold. He intends to pray for Martin, for he does not know whether Marshal Dale will agree.

Fare thee well my dearest friend,

Abigail

London, England

Dear Abigail,

I have such wondrous news! Papa and Mother and I have all been invited to attend the wedding of Princess Elizabeth to Frederick V. She will be the Queen of Bohemia when he becomes King. They are getting married on Valentine's Day next month. Isn't that delightfully romantic? Princess Elizabeth is only fifteen. I cannot even imagine myself married yet.

The news gets even better. There are many celebrations and festivities surrounding the wedding. You'll never guess . . . one of the festivities is a performance of *The Tempest*! By the King's Men! At the Globe Theater! And I will be attending with Papa! Just like he promised. We are going together with Sir Henry Wriothesley, the Earl of Southampton, Shakespeare's dearest patron and friend. I cannot wait to tell you everything about it. Oh, Abigail, I do wish you were here to share this with me. We would have such fun shopping for shoes and clothing. Mother says I may have two new dresses. Of course, the one for the wedding must be just right. I think Mother thinks I will meet a potential future husband at the wedding. She is clucking and fussing with fabrics, brocades, and materials and talking with the tailor at least twice a day. I am to have both dresses made and there is not that much time.

Two days have passed since I started this letter. It was cold today, but not rainy, so Mother and I went shopping at the Royal Exchange. The most wondrous items are for sale there. We bought fabric, buttons, and new shoes for the festivities. The tailor comes in a few days to begin the work on our dresses. My dress will be a brilliant blue satin with an ivory brocade jacket. Mother has chosen an emerald green for her dress. This is so exciting. A royal wedding!

I must go, for Mother is calling me for another fitting. I promise to tell you every detail.

Your friend,

Elizabeth

Rock Hall

January 10, 1613

Dear Elizabeth,

Oh how I hate stitchery. I didn't mind the simple sewing of James Towne. After all, we had to make shirts for our valiant soldiers. It is this fancy stitchery that makes me so frustrated. I find my fingers tangle up the yarn before it can even reach the cloth. I am sure, my dear Elizabeth, that your needlework is extraordinary. Mine is extraordinarily horrible. Will I ever be properly readied for marriage when I cannot do the simplest of tasks assigned to the female? The Rock Hall church ladies who instruct me in needlework assure me that it will not always be so. Today, however, I think even they were taxed with my latest effort.

While stitching today, Mrs. Harvey spoke of the grand reception among the men of Master Rolfe's new tobacco blend. Have you heard of it? He has been experimenting the last several years, but this time, he took seeds from the West Indies and crossed them with seeds from some of his earlier tobacco experiments. The men here enjoy it, that I do know. There are great hopes that tobacco can become the staple crop that provides the Virginia Company with its long-awaited profit. Tell your father that the men here say Master Rolfe's tobacco is sweet and pleasant.

The church ladies also said there were not many of us left. I had not realized so many had died. The ladies spoke of how they felt safe here at Rock Hall because it is surrounded by five forts. They spoke quietly around me, Elizabeth, but I think they were talking about Indian raids.

The women spoke again of the Indian Princess Pocahontas. It is strange that we have heard nothing from her these last few years since the return of Henry Spelman. I prefer the little princess stay far, far away, so it is just as well that no one has seen her.

I must put down my quill now, Elizabeth. My fingers are so tired from stitching that I cannot write any more tonight.

Faithfully,

Abigail

London, England

February 10, 1613

Dearest Abigail,

I was so deeply moved last evening after the performance of *The Tempest* that I wasn't sure I would be able to write you everything I wanted to say. Then I woke up this morning and could not wait to pick up my quill, dip it in the ink, and tell you every detail.

Papa and I took a boat across the River Thames to the Globe Theater. There we met Sir Henry Wriothesley, Earl of Southampton. He guided us to wonderful seats, where I could see the entire stage. The very first scene is the hurricane on the sea. The ship tossed to and fro in the gale winds seemed so real, it was hard to believe I was watching a play on a stage. I sat on the edge of my seat the entire time.

Miranda said at the very end, "O wonder! How many goodly creatures are there here! How beauteous mankind is! O brave new world that has such people in it!" You, my dearest friend, are in that brave New World with many different kinds of people. You, my dear friend, have been hurt deeply by those different people. Perhaps the people there, the Indians, are "goodly creatures" and "beauteous." I know you must be thinking that's easy for me to say. Yet, after watching the play, I could not help but think that there is a wondrous mystery in your life there in the brave new world of Virginia that has a deeper meaning still.

Sir Henry was quite entertaining. He explained to me that Shakespeare had read every word William Strachey had written in his report of the shipwreck. After seeing the play, I want to read Master Strachey's report as well and compare the two. Abigail, you lived through that amazing hurricane, and the play brought it so very much alive to me. I am even more in awe of how God must have his hand on you, dear friend. There has been a sea change in your life these last few years, but there is something "beauteous" that is going to come out it. I just know it.

Your friend,

Elizabeth

London, England

February 15, 1613

Dear Abigail,

Oh, how I wish you could have been with me yesterday for the royal wedding. I wish you could have been here for the entire week. There have been festivities and fireworks. The most glorious fireworks were last night as ships gathered on the River Thames to salute the new couple. I have hardly slept all week.

Papa, Mother, John, and I gathered with some friends from the Virginia Company and went together to the wedding. The royal carriage brought the princess through the streets of London so everyone could wave and wish her well. We went to Westminster Abbey for the wedding ceremony. We then took a boat down the River Thames to the palace for the feast and dance. Never have I seen so many beautiful maidens (and handsome men!) in one place. I danced all the night long until Papa insisted we go home. Mother's feet hurt, but I could have danced until morning.

Your exhausted and very happy friend,

Elizabeth

Rock Hall

February 21, 1613

Dearest Elizabeth,

Reverend Whitaker and I had the discussion again. You know, dear Elizabeth, that he wants me to forgive those who have wronged me. He wants me to forgive the Indians for taking Mother and Father away from me. I will not! We seem never to resolve the matter. I would rather not discuss it, but he seems determined to "get to the heart of the matter," as he says. Why won't he just leave it alone? It stirs me all up inside, Elizabeth, so much so that I will not write another word tonight.

*Good night,
my dear friend,*

Abigail

London, England

March 14, 1613

Dear Abigail,

Papa says that Reverend Whitaker's report, *Good News from Virginia,* has stirred many hearts here in England. Reverend Whitaker challenged us to help the colonists in Virginia. I hope his good words help. I am afraid those Indian raids and the starving time did not do much for the new colony's image, and many of the original stockholders were very disappointed that Virginia did not yield the gold ore they had hoped it would.

Papa says they are taking new subscriptions for stock in the Company, and although they are coming in slowly, he is encouraged. They may send new settlers soon. Papa wants people to see it as Reverend Whitaker does—a great opportunity to participate in something God is doing. Papa says that sometimes people can't see the amazing things God wants them to participate in with him because they are too busy pursuing their own interests.

I know, dear Abigail, that you want to see what God is doing right there at Rock Hall.

Your friend,

Elizabeth

Rock Hall

April 20, 1613

Dearest Elizabeth,

How delighted I was to get your letters. I did not know that the Company was prepared to send more settlers to Virginia. When are they due to arrive? Will they have a pair of boots for me?

As much as I adore the generous gifts your mother and father showered upon me, a pair of sturdy boots would serve me well. Please do pass on to them the enclosed letter of thanks for their gifts and love.

Elizabeth, I can hardly imagine your life now. Balls and dancing, royal weddings, Shakespearean theater at the Globe, dresses of satin and brocade. It all seems so far away. My life is so different from yours. And yet, if the church ladies have their way, a proper English lady I will yet become.

Today I was schooled in my recipe book. I think this is entirely silly. I am made to copy recipes for every manner of food that is entirely unavailable in this country. It is as if I am being schooled to be a young English woman in London with you. But we do not eat mutton or beef here. We eat wild turkey, deer, corn, fish, and even oysters from the river. I know what you are thinking, Elizabeth. You are wondering how I would deign to eat oysters. You think them beneath our station, I know. Oh, how good oysters taste though, when there are no finer delicacies to be had. Most of our meals are pottage stew.

It was utter torture to copy the recipe for gingerbread. Oh, how I do miss my sweets here in this new world. I think that is the greatest hardship of all—no gingerbread!

I will have to introduce you to the finer things the New World has to offer. Perhaps you will come to visit one day, Elizabeth. Tell your father to send you over on the next ship! You will probably simply marry a fine Oxford man and be done with your old friend, Abigail. There are Oxford men here too, Elizabeth! Come to visit! I will show you how to eat oysters, and you can take a special oyster stew recipe back to copy in your recipe book. Now, Elizabeth, think it not beneath your station to consume such a delicacy of the New World! Adventure calls here, Elizabeth. I am sure the Indians will be kinder to you than they have been to me.

Your obedient servant,

Abigail

P.S. News has come that Pocahontas has been captured by Captain Argall and brought back to James Towne. Surely Chief Powhatan will kill us all now!

Rock Hall

May 3, 1613

Dear Elizabeth,

    I heard Reverend Whitaker talking with Marshal Dale today. It seems that a ransom demand was issued to Chief Powhatan. We will return his daughter, the Princess Pocahontas, to him upon the return of our swords and guns and seven men who were captured a while ago. We are also asking for a great quantity of corn. There has been no word from Chief Powhatan.

    I am not walking Reverend Whitaker's farm as I used to do. I know we are many miles away from James Towne, but I am still very much afraid. Elizabeth, I can hardly sleep at night. The sounds of the night are like those I used to hear outside the James Towne fort during the starving time. Are the Powhatan Indians lying in the grass waiting to attack?

Frightened,

Abigail

Rock Hall

May 24, 1613

Dear Elizabeth,

I am furious with Reverend Whitaker. He has agreed to keep the Princess Pocahontas here at Rock Hall! Apparently, there has still been no word from Chief Powhatan. Marshal Dale thinks that the Princess will be safer here at Rock Hall because of the fortifications surrounding Reverend Whitaker's farm. There are more soldiers here and better armor and weapons. It does not appear that Chief Powhatan is going to respond to the demands any time soon, so they need a place for the Princess to live and learn about God. Why? The Princess Pocahontas has her own gods she can worship. Why does she need my God?

Reverend Whitaker is thrilled. I will have to take my lessons with her for he is most heartily encouraged that he finally has a savage to convert to the faith. He wants her to study Scripture right along with me, and he also wants me to teach her the ways of the English. Imagine!

I am definitely not interested in what God is doing here anymore. No, sir. He can win the Princess Pocahontas to himself, but he can do it without me. I told Mrs. Sizemore that I will not attend the catechism class, and I don't care what Marshal Dale does to me.

In fact, I am not sure the God of the English could be God to these pagan Indians all at the same time. Not when the Indians killed my father and mother.

I am so furious. I will write no more tonight or I may say things to you, dear Elizabeth, that I will regret, and you, my dearest friend, have done nothing to deserve my ire. I doubt I will get any sleep tonight. The Indian Princess is to arrive tomorrow.

Your friend,

Abigail

Rock Hall

May 25, 1613

Dear Elizabeth,

Mrs. Sizemore and some of the other church ladies spent the morning preparing for the arrival of Princess Pocahontas. If you ask me, they overdid it. Breads, meats, and even sweets! Mrs. Sizemore used our special spices and sugar to make gingerbread. Gingerbread for the Princess! In May! Why, they are wasting our special Christmas treat on her! Other church ladies were up early in the morning, taking the napkins off the napkin press and setting the table board for the noonday meal. Some were preparing the Princess's room that, dear Elizabeth, is right next to mine! I will keep my door locked every night.

Mrs. Sizemore directed everyone in their duties and twittered about, clucking disapproval for any little thing out of place. She asked me to help, but I refused. She complained to Reverend Whitaker, but I overhead him tell her to let me be. Thank the Lord for that bit of grace. I stayed in my room and sat by the window, watching for the Princess to arrive.

I tried to read my Bible, Father's Bible, but the sorrow inside nearly overwhelmed me. I miss Father and Mother so very much. My heart twisted and turned inside my chest with the pain caused by the thoughts of my parents. I may be a nearly grown woman (after all, I will be sixteen soon), but I just wish I could rest my head in Mother's lap one more time and hear her soothe away all my worries and troubles. Mother always knew exactly what to do and what to say. Oh, Elizabeth, what will I say to this Princess Pocahontas?

Mrs. Sizemore is thrilled to be meeting the Princess. Many have told stories about what she did to help this colony and the English, but few English are left who remember her. Mrs. Sizemore told me that Pocahontas saved the English from certain death several times.

I am glad Reverend Whitaker is leaving me alone now. I would much rather write to you than fuss with preparations for the beloved Princess. She may have saved other lives, but there is nothing she did to prevent my mother from starving or my father from being killed by her people. Others may adore her. I do not.

Your friend,

Abigail

Rock Hall

May 26, 1613

Dear Elizabeth,

Marshal Dale arrived with the Princess about 1:00 in the afternoon in time for the meal. With him were Governor Thomas Gates, Reverend Richard Bucke, Master John Rolfe, and Master Ralph Hamor. To my great surprise and delight, Captain Pierce also came. Captain Pierce seemed to know I needed him, and he stayed close beside me all afternoon. He sat with me at our meal that, thankfully, I was able to take in another room. All the important men of the colony ate with the Princess. Actually, I felt a bit sorry for her having to dine with all those men and with Mrs. Sizemore clucking around tending to her every need.

Captain Pierce caught me up on all the news of Mistress Pierce and Jane. Mistress Pierce still has the best garden in the colony, but Captain Pierce says his wife hears that my garden may one day rival hers. He winked at me, as we both know that will never happen. No matter how good a gardener I become, no one can match Mistress Pierce. I told him that I was planting figs this year, just as I had watched Mistress Pierce do. Captain Pierce said that in his life he has not seen two women who so greatly love to sink their hands into the warm dirt, and never did he imagine that he would have the privilege of loving them both. When I asked him who those women were, he said, "Why Mistress Pierce and you, of course!" I blushed, for I had quite forgotten how good God was to me, providing me with such loving friends of my parents to care for me when I was distressed. Why, they have really adopted me into their family and made me one of their own.

Captain Pierce continued, "Abigail, I know this is difficult for you. I know having Pocahontas here brings back painful memories you have tried so hard to forget. Mistress Pierce and I are praying for you. We know that God is going to work much good out of this, and we believe that he has a purpose for you to be in the Princess's life." I must have looked very surprised because Captain Pierce continued, "Mistress Pierce and I were very saddened when it was decided that you should come to Rock Hall, for you are one of our family. We could see the wisdom of the Council in providing you with proper instruction in the Bible, reviving your formal schooling, and proper instruction in English and womanly ways. We know the plans they have in Henricus for a college and a school. There are many women here involved with Reverend Whitaker's church who could instruct you in many areas you will need if you are to be one of the best New World women possible. In not too many years, you will be married and having children of your own.

"We know Reverend Whitaker and his heart, and we know that your Father and Mother would have approved. That is why, although we were saddened, we were able to give our blessing to these plans. We are apart now, but we are never far away. We think of you every day and pray for you each night. You are very special, Abigail, and God has his hand on your life. Do not fear the strange twist of circumstances that seems to have come upon you. There is a reason and a purpose. Do not run away in your heart and turn your back on his mysterious ways. You may experience a miracle of his grace."

I hugged Captain Pierce tightly and several tears slid down my face. I do so miss him and Mistress Pierce and little Jane. They had been so faithful to take me in when I was without Mother and Father. I am not sure I understand his words to me, but they were soothing and somehow in my spirit, they brought comfort. For his sake, I will try to bear this terrible burden of the Princess Pocahontas in my life.

After their meal, the gentlemen retired to the parlor to discuss the situation with the ransom demand. Reverend Whitaker brought the Princess Pocahontas to me. My heart was beating very fast. Captain Pierce gave me a kiss on the cheek and gave me a little nudge over to where the Princess stood before he joined the other men. The two of us just stared at each other for what seemed like a very long time.

Pocahontas was dressed like me. Gone were the deerskin clothes of the Indian girls. Instead, she was covered head to toe in linen—skirt, bodice, and petticoat. Were it not for her dark skin and strange haircut, she could have been just any other English girl in the New World.

Reverend Whitaker said, "Why don't you show the Princess your garden?" I looked at him in surprise, and said,

"Outside?" Reverend Whitaker laughed, and said, "The Princess is to have freedom within bounds here at Rock Hall, Abigail. Surely on such a lovely day as this, and after such a long journey by ship up the James River, she would enjoy being in the sunshine with you." Well, that certainly sounded like a good idea to me. I didn't want to stay inside a moment longer. Reverend Whitaker took two straw hats down from the pegged board near the door and handed one to the Princess and one to me. We looked at each other. I did not want to be with the Princess, but I did want to be outside. Princess Pocahontas smiled. I put on my hat and tied the ribbons under my chin in a bow. Pocahontas watched and copied what I did, although her bow looked more like a knot to me. Reverend Whitaker opened the door and within seconds, we were both outdoors in the sunshine, like two prisoners set free.

For a few minutes, Pocahontas just stood with her face lifted to the warm sun. She closed her eyes and seemed to bask in its warmth. Then she opened her eyes, smiled, and said, "Garden?" I was surprised. I had no idea she could speak any English. We walked over to my garden. I pointed out to her the different plants I had planted. I showed her my beans, squash, turnips, potatoes, and flowers. It was the flowers that seemed to interest Pocahontas most. She would turn a quizzical face to me as she lifted the flower gently with her fingers. Each time, I would tell her what the flower was. Each time she would repeat the word. I was surprised at how quickly she learned the names of the flowers.

Pocahontas squatted down and put both hands in the dirt that had been warmed by the sun. She closed her eyes again as if she were remembering something. She let the warm dirt fall between her fingers for several minutes before she tried to stand up. When she did attempt to stand, her right foot stepped on her petticoat, and she tripped and fell in the dirt. She tried to get up again and stepped on another part of her petticoat and fell again. I tried hard not to laugh as, after all, she is a princess. But when it happened a third time, I laughed so hard I clutched my apron and wiped away the tears. Then I realized what I had done— laughing at a Princess! I probably had offended her. I looked down in horror at her as she sat in the dirt, and she smiled at me. Then she began to laugh too. She reached up her hand for me to help her. I showed her how to hike up her skirts, and then I grabbed her outreached hand and helped her up. She said, "Thank you," and then haltingly added, "Abigail." I was surprised at how well she could com- municate. I had heard Reverend Whitaker tell Mrs. Sizemore that she was quite facile with our language from her time with Captain John Smith and Henry Spelman, but it still surprised me. She dusted herself off just as Mrs. Sizemore began to call for us.

When we got inside, I took off my hat and hung it on the peg. I helped Pocahantas with the knot she had tied. When looking in her eyes, I saw a mixture of curiosity and something else—was it sorrow? Mrs. Sizemore soon scuttled her off to meet the other church ladies. There was more clucking over the Princess as they showed her the room, clothes, shoes, and books for school that they had prepared for her. A Bible was placed prominently next to her bed. I wondered, since the Princess could speak English, whether she could read and write it?

As the ladies took Pocahontas on a tour of the parsonage, I had an idea. I went back out to the garden and cut a bouquet of flowers. I filled a leather jug with water from the spring and put the flowers in it. I moved the Bible on her table over just a bit and placed the jug of flowers next to her bed. I think she will enjoy them. I know I do.

That evening Reverend Whitaker spent some time speaking with Pocahontas, but Mrs. Sizemore made short order of that as well. "The child must get her rest, Reverend," she said sternly. Never one to cross Mrs. Sizemore, Reverend Whitaker prayed that Pocahontas would sleep well and that God would watch over her and lead her to himself. No sooner had he said his "Amen," than Mrs. Sizemore had Pocahontas by the hand and was leading her off to bed. I could imagine Pocahontas being schooled by Mrs. Sizemore in nighttime rituals. I had to laugh thinking of the woman trying to show Pocahontas how to use a chamber pot. The church ladies now have a project—and a grand one it is. Poor Pocahontas!

So glad to be an ordinary English girl in the New World, Elizabeth, I remain

Your friend,

Abigail

Rock Hall

June 1, 1613

Dear Elizabeth,

I must hurry. Reverend Whitaker will take my letters to the *Elizabeth.* Captain Adams leaves in a few days for London and will make sure my letters get to you. My letters to my dearest Elizabeth will arrive in just seven weeks on the *Elizabeth.* I pretend the ship was named for you.

Perhaps it is a good thing Pocahontas has someone close to her age here. Reverend Whitaker tells me she is about seventeen years old. I have hardly seen her this week. The church ladies have made her their project. They took her to visit other ladies of the colony.

They all want to have some part in turning the Indian Princess into an English lady. Reverend Whitaker thinks that in several weeks the novelty will wear off and we will be able to get back to a routine here. Reverend Whitaker wants to begin our catechism lessons shortly. I am to join the class with the Princess.

Reverend Whitaker thinks it will be a grand idea to invite Master Rolfe to come by to read to the Princess from the Bible. Apparently, although she can converse in English better than expected, she has no knowledge of the written English word. Reverend Whitaker said he can use all the help he can get since being able to read God's Word for oneself is needful for a Christian. I suppose he has high hopes she will forgo her heathen ways and accept the English God.

I am not so sure.

I must go now. Reverend Whitaker is leaving. I will tie this bundle of letters together right away. I miss you, dear Elizabeth. I long to hear from you. Soon I will have word from you as I have heard a delivery ship is due to arrive next month.

Your friend,

Abigail

Rock Hall

June 15, 1613

Dear Elizabeth,

The Princess is to attend church twice daily with me. On Sunday morning, we are to attend church service and catechism class together. The special teachings that Reverend Whitaker gives at Marshal Dale's home will be every Saturday night. Master Rolfe and Master Hamor both attend those meetings. The Princess may not participate in the monthly communion as she does not have understanding of what it means, but Reverend Whitaker wants her to attend so she can listen and learn.

Even with all this instruction in the ways of God, Reverend Whitaker wants to have a special catechism class with just the Princess and me. He thinks that she will feel freer to ask questions if it is just the three of us.

Today, he asked Pocahontas the names of her gods. She told him that Ahone is the creator god and Okee is the devil god. She shivered when she mentioned Okee. "Tell me about Ahone," asked Reverend Whitaker.

"Ahone is creator god. Like the sun, he gives all that is good. But he is not as powerful as Okee. Okee is devil god.

Okee makes us sick. Okee destroys our corn. Okee sends storms and fire to ruin our land."

"How do you make Okee stop doing those things?" asked Reverend Whitaker.

Pocahontas just turned her head. I saw a tear slide down her cheek. She said, "Sacrifice."

Reverend Whitaker told her that the God of the English is merciful and just, loving and good. He said that nothing evil or destructive can come from him.

"Then he must be weak, like Ahone," said Pocahontas.

"Sometimes, what appears to be weak is really strong," replied Reverend Whitaker. "Sometimes what seems like defeat is really victory. I will tell you more later, but for now, Pocahontas, know that the English God is called Father by his Son, Jesus, and Jesus taught us that when we pray, we are also to call him Father."

Pocahontas seemed upset at the mention of the word "Father." When Reverend Whitaker ended his lesson, Pocahontas opened the door and went for a walk. I followed her. Pocahontas went to my garden! She knelt down in the warm dirt and sobbed. I heard her utter only one word. "Father!" she said through her tears. Did she mean Father God or her father? I didn't know what to say to her, so I quietly slipped away and let her be alone.

Your confused friend,

Abigail

Rock Hall

June 22, 1613

Dear Elizabeth,

Marshal Dale arrived today to speak with Reverend Whitaker, and he brought him a present—a horse! There are only six horses in the colony, so Reverend Whitaker was very surprised. Reverend Whitaker has many people in his parish to visit, and Marshal Dale wanted him to be able to get around faster. He also gave us a cart for the horse to pull. This will make it easier for the three of us to attend the Saturday evening Bible classes at Marshal Dale's home.

As we admired Reverend Whitaker's fine new horse, I noticed that Pocahontas seemed at ease with the beast, even though she has never ridden one. I think growing up around so many animals puts her at ease. I do regret not being schooled in horsemanship as you are, dear Elizabeth. If I had remained in England, I should have taken lessons with you at your summer home. It seems to me that such lessons would come in handy now that we have a horse. Reverend Whitaker thanked Marshal Dale for such a valuable gift. Reverend Whitaker asked me if I would be willing to care for the horse. We named him Admiral (after Admiral

Somers)—a most commanding name for a strong, commanding horse.

Reverend Whitaker told Marshal Dale that the Princess was very quiet but seemed to be taking her lessons in English reading and writing well. As to her interest in the English God, he was not so sure. He told Marshal Dale that he was glad for the help of others such as Master Rolfe, who comes weekly to read to her from the Bible.

The Princess came into the room to boldly ask Marshal Dale if there had been any news from her father, Chief Powhatan. He said there had been no response at all to their demand for a ransom for her return. The Princess turned abruptly so they could not see her face. But I saw it.

I followed her to her room as she threw herself on the bed and cried. *Ah ha! Her father does not want her back! That is why she is so distressed*, I thought. *That is what she meant by "Father" in the garden.* She may be a princess, but she is not wanted by her own father, not more than his precious guns and weapons and corn.

I suppose I took some pleasure in the fact that her father had abandoned her. After all, it was at her father's orders that we received no corn or help in any way and my mother starved. It was at her father's orders that my father was killed by an arrow from one of his tribe's weapons. I felt a little guilty, but not much. I do not think it is right to try to tell Pocahontas about our God. The Indians have their own gods. Let Pocahontas pray to Okee and Ahone now to help her.

When Marshal Dale left, I asked Reverend Whitaker, "Chief Powhatan is not going to bargain for his daughter, is he?"

"No, it does not look like he will," answered the Reverend.

"Then your project is meaningless. If Pocahontas is not going to go back to her tribe, then what use is it to teach her about our God? She won't be able to share it with anyone else."

"Abigail, you surprise me. You profess to know and love God, and yet you seem not to understand his heart. Do you not recall the passage in the gospel of John that says God loves the world so much that he desires not one person to perish. He said anyone who believes in him will not perish but will have everlasting life. Did God mean only the English?"

Perhaps, I thought. I will not get into this discussion again with Reverend Whitaker. We simply disagree on whether the Indians should know about our God. He says that all men need to know of the grace and mercy of God and the sacrifice he made for us. I say things are fine the way they are. The Indians are happy with their gods. Why, they even have two gods, not one like us. Let them be.

Elizabeth, there is a strange tugging at my heart, and I know not what it is. Reverend Whitaker says it is the Holy Spirit trying to instruct me of my own sin of bitterness and hatred of people God made in his own image. I think not. I will do what I have done in the past when this tugging comes. I will ignore it.

Your friend,

Abigail

Rock Hall

July 5, 1613

Dear Elizabeth,

Incredible news. Chief Powhatan finally sent a messenger to Marshal Dale. He is willing to pay the ransom. There is to be a bargain. Perhaps Pocahontas will return to her father and no longer live at Rock Hall! I ran to give Pocahontas the good news. I found her digging in the garden—my garden. She is not supposed to dirty her hands with work like that. After all, she is royalty, and the church ladies have tried these last few weeks to get that idea through her head. Well, this will be the last day she will be in my garden. She will no longer be our hostage and will be free to return to her people.

I told the Princess that her father had finally spoken. He sent back with the messenger seven of the English captives. "And the weapons?" the Princess inquired.

"I didn't hear anything about any weapons," I replied. Her face darkened. "What's the matter, Pocahontas? Shouldn't you be rejoicing? Your father has met the demands."

"Father has only met part of the demands, Abigail. The other part of the ransom demanded by Marshal Dale was the return of all the weapons our people have taken from the English over the years. I know father will never give those up."

"Don't be discouraged. Come. Let's go and find out. I am sure he sent weapons with the men as well."

We hurried back to the parsonage where Marshal Dale, Governor Gates, and Reverend Whitaker had gathered. We heard Marshal Dale say, "This is outrageous. He sends a broken musket with each of the men. He is taunting us. We must hold her until he has paid the full ransom. She is being well cared for here."

Governor Gates replied, "Ah, yes, that is what I was afraid of. Chief Powhatan knows we will not harm her so he will simply bide his time. I agree, we cannot release her now. The idea that he does not know where the weapons are is preposterous. We must have the weapons or Princess Pocahontas will never go home to her father."

I stole a glance at Pocahontas. She understood most of what Marshal Dale and Governor Gates were saying. She knew she was not going home that day. I don't know who was more disappointed—Pocahontas or me.

Reverend Whitaker noted that her lessons in the Bible were going very well and, with the help of John Rolfe, her reading and writing of the English language would increase as well. "Several more months of her living here and learning of God's love for her would be more than acceptable to me," he offered.

Suddenly, Pocahontas slipped outside, hiked up her skirts, and ran as fast as the wind. She ran and ran so that I could not keep up with her. She finally came to a large oak tree with thick and strong branches. Then she scrambled up the branches, skirts and all. She was sobbing so hard I don't think she heard me coming, even though I was breathing hard and fast from running after her. She spoke both in her native language and in English. Her English is better than she lets on. I think she is smarter than us all. I could understand every word she was saying and she spoke with passion and a good command of our language. I wonder why she pretends her lessons with Master Rolfe are going so slowly?

Elizabeth, she cried out that her father had abandoned her. She spoke how she was his favorite daughter—his little Snow Feather. "Many times when my father had to bargain for other captives," said Pocahontas, "he gladly gave up weapons and other valuable items to redeem his warriors. Am I not as valuable to him as they? Does not my father love me anymore?" Her heart was breaking and she cried many tears. She cried so loudly from the bottom of her soul that I realized she had no idea I was there. I slipped away.

I had seen part of the Princess's heart that she never intended for me to see. She too loves her father very much and misses him. As I do mine. That strange tugging is in my heart again.

Your friend,

Abigail

Rock Hall

August 20, 1613

Dear Elizabeth,

Today, Pocahontas and I walked in the garden. I cut some flowers for the parsonage. Then I heard Pocahontas gasp. There was Henry Spelman! Pocahontas threw her arms around him and began chattering to him in her native language, while Henry chattered back. Henry had done a good job learning her language for the several years they were together. Henry and Pocahontas walked and talked together for a long time.

Later that night, Henry explained to me that the Princess is very distressed that her father has refused to redeem her by paying the full ransom the English require. He had done nothing for three months and even then released seven men who came back with broken muskets. Marshal Dale refuses to release Pocahontas until the Chief meets all of his demands. Pocahontas is determined to be patient though.

Devotedly,

Abigail

London, England

June 24, 1613

Dear Abigail,

The Globe Theater burned down yesterday! The wondrous theater where Shakespeare has had so many of his plays performed is now just ashes and rubble. Last night there was a performance of his play *Henry VIII*. A cannon was fired as is supposed to be done during the play, and the flaming cannonball shot out of the cannon and landed on top of a thatched roof. The entire theater burned to the ground in only two hours. Everyone escaped with their lives, however.

I am so glad I saw *The Tempest* there just a few months ago.

Papa told me that is how the first fire at James Towne started before you ever arrived. Those thatched roofs keep out the rain very well, but certainly not the fire.

Your friend,

Elizabeth

London, England

July 25, 1613

Dear Abigail,

Your letters arrived today with news of the capture of Pocahontas. All London is astir with the news. I knew I must write quickly. Another ship is due to sail in three days, so I will bring the letter to the Captain myself.

Forgive me if I sound harsh. But Abigail, you are just not thinking clearly. There have been many reports here of the number of Indians the English have killed. Those dead Indians were someone's mother or father or sister or brother. Why do you think God is only interested in being the God of the English? Where in the Bible do you read that, dear friend?

Dear Abigail, think. What have you been taught all your life about our God? That God so loved the world he gave his only Son, Jesus, so that anyone who believed in him would not perish, but have eternal life. Did Jesus come only to save the English? I fear your emotions will cause you great trouble there. You must think!

Concerned,

Elizabeth

Rock Hall

September 4, 1613

Dear Elizabeth,

I just finished reading your letters. You too! Are you and Reverend Whitaker in cahoots with one another? Now you are both quoting the same Bible passage to me. I will not hold it against you, dear friend, but I simply do not agree. I did have that strange tugging in my heart again as I read your letter, though. I promise I will think about what you have said. Perhaps it would be best if I read that passage in the gospel of John again too. I am not changing my thinking, mind you, but I promise I will at least ponder it more.

John Rolfe comes around more and more these days. I don't mind, though, for he often brings his friend Master Robert Sparkes. Master Sparkes talks with me while Master Rolfe reads to Pocahontas and helps her with her reading and writing from the hornbook. I don't dare let on that I know her English speaking is much better than Master Rolfe imagines. I wonder if the Princess likes him to come to see her so she pretends her lessons are going much slower than they really are. She is very clever!

Master Sparkes is a very interesting young man. He is nineteen, Elizabeth, and I would put him up as a match for any of those young college men you are with at your fancy parties. He was in the midst of his course of study at Cambridge when he met Reverend Whitaker. It was Reverend Whitaker's passion for this New World that stirred his interest. He began to consider coming to the New World before he had finished his university training. Reverend Whitaker encouraged him to stay a few more years and finish his course work, but Master Sparkes had too much adventure in him to stay.

He likes to come to Reverend Whitaker's parsonage, though, and look through his library. The Reverend has been very good about loaning him books. I look forward to the wonderful packages your family sends me. Reverend Whitaker walks around whistling for weeks after he gets a package from his father or his brother, Jabez. His package is always full of books.

Master Sparkes has blond hair and blue eyes that sparkle when he laughs. He has determined to help Master Rolfe with this next crop of tobacco. He thinks Master Rolfe is one of the hardest workers he has ever known. Master Rolfe is determined to keep up his experiments until he finds the right blend of seeds and the best process for curing the tobacco leaves. He wants to make a crop that will cause London to be thankful it has a colony in America. Have you heard anything about the first crop he sent over this summer? Would you ask your father? This supply ship brought no news about his tobacco. This is unfortunate, because Master Rolfe is at work on harvesting his next crop even now.

Today, after our lessons, we went to Master Rolfe's fields. Reverend Whitaker smiled his blessing on us, and even offered us his horse, while Mrs. Sizemore clucked her disapproval. She would much rather have the Princess and me working on needlework with her church ladies. Of course, Pocahontas and I are always happy when we are outside or in a garden. The Princess knows much about tobacco, at least the Indian kind. Master Rolfe says it is much too bitter for the English taste, but he is interested in what Pocahontas knows about growing tobacco in Virginia soil.

The Princess spent many hours in his fields moving among his tobacco plants. She carefully examined the plants and the coloring of the leaves. She felt the leaves between her fingers, crushed some of the leaves, and then smelled the aroma they released. She was very serious and contemplative. Sometimes she would crush the tobacco leaves and smell them while her eyes were closed and her face was lifted to the warming sun. Master Sparkes explained to me that knowing when to harvest is equally as important as what kind of tobacco seeds to plant. Harvesting plants too early or too late can ruin the crop. The Princess smiled at Master Rolfe and said in her best English, "It is time."

Master Sparkes said he would escort us back to the parsonage, but we assured him we could make it back ourselves. Besides, both Pocahontas and I knew what we wanted to do. We wanted to see how fast Admiral could run. We both sat on Admiral in our most ladylike manner, side-saddle, skirts pulled up modestly covering our legs, the way an English lady rides. We gently prodded Admiral to walk slowly down the road as we waved—oh, so ladylike—to Master Rolfe and Master Sparkes. Then, as soon as we were out of their sight, we straddled Admiral, kicked his sides, and hung on for dear life. Admiral seemed to sense our need for freedom and ran like the wind. We leaned low over Admiral's neck and clung to the reins and his mane. It was glorious and both Pocahontas and I laughed with joy as we rode back to the parsonage. A few miles before the parsonage, we slowed down and walked Admiral the rest of the way home so he could cool down.

We were quiet for a while. Then Pocahontas said, "Abigail, I know that you do not like me. I do not know why." She let the sentence hang there for a minute. It was more a statement than a question and yet, I knew she deserved an answer. But was this the time? I could not decide whether to answer her or not. I spent so much time thinking about it that I was surprised to realize we were back at Rock Hall. Pocahontas slipped off Admiral and went inside the parsonage. I dismounted and took Admiral's reins and walked him to the barn. The entire time I brushed Admiral down, I could not stop thinking about what Pocahontas had said. I put Admiral's blanket on him, gave him water, and then closed the stall gate.

Pocahontas sat quietly in the library all evening while Reverend Whitaker read to her from the Bible. I felt too guilty to be in the same room with her and went to bed early. Elizabeth, I do not know what to say to her. I do not like her. She knows it, and I know it.

Your troubled friend,

Abigail

157

London, England

September 20, 1613

Dear Abigail,

Papa and Mother have hired a dancing instructor, Master Peppe, who is to teach me. Papa and Mother plan for me to accompany them this year to all of the holiday balls and parties. Mother says it is time for me to be courted by a proper English gentleman. I am nearly sixteen, and Mother seems very preoccupied with marrying me off.

Master Peppe kept clapping his hands in time with the music, but my feet would not cooperate. It was a disaster. He rolled his eyes, threw up his hands, and told Mother he would return next week. Mother fretted that I will not be ready for the Christmas balls. I just wanted to hop on the next ship and come visit you. Life was so simple until now.

Of course, after reading your letters, I realize your life is anything but simple. You have much that weighs on your heart, and it is not the frivolity of dancing lessons. However, I do detect that you, too, may soon be courted by that young Master Sparkes. Of course, I have learned he is a gentle soul with a quick wit and a heart full of adventure. I strongly suspect you already know that.

Your clumsy friend,

Elizabeth

London, England

September 29, 1613

Dear Abigail,

Today a new Lord Mayor was elected. He is a good friend of Papa's. His name is Thomas Middleton. Do you remember meeting him years ago? He is a member of the Virginia Company, but I do not think that is what gives him his popularity. Today, Michaelmas Day in 1613, will go down in history as the day London got fresh drinking water! And whom do we have to thank? The Right Honorable Lord Mayor's brother, Hugh Middleton.

Today the Lord Mayor performed the opening ceremony. When he turned the wheel at the reservoir, he cried out, "Flow forth precious spring!" To the sound of the fanfare of trumpets, water came rushing through to London. Papa says it is amazing what the Lord Mayor's brother has done in four years to build a New River. The channel of aqueducts takes pure water from Hertfordshire and moves it across 40 miles and 100 wooden bridges as it dips and winds its way to London. Papa says that once the water gets to the New River head in Clerkenwell in London, it pours into pipes made of hollowed elm trees and is piped into different parts of London. We are thrilled now to have clean water come directly to our homes. Hooray for Hugh Middleton. Hooray for clean water!

No longer will we have to buy our water from the Honorable Company of Water Tankard Bearers who Papa says always overcharged. No longer will our water be polluted. I can't wait to taste the clean, fresh water that will come right into the cistern at our home. Do you know, Abigail, I have never asked you how you get your water in Virginia. I assume you have no Honorable Company of Water Tankard Bearers to bring water to your home. What do you do? Sometimes, I forget that you are worlds away with a very different life.

Here's to a clean mug of water!

Your no longer thirsty friend,

Elizabeth

Rock Hall

October 6, 1613

Dear Elizabeth,

We did not see much of either Master Rolfe or Master Sparkes during September. They were busy harvesting Master Rolfe's tobacco crop. The tobacco leaves are curing under hay now. Pocahontas suggested Master Rolfe dry the leaves hung over sticks rather than leave them in heaps on the ground. He is not sure about this method, but is trying it. He seems to respect her and her people's ways. He doesn't seem to hold any grudges against the Indians. In fact, he seems to have a respect for Pocahontas's knowledge of agriculture—a respect he gives to her despite the fact that she is a woman.

I think he is sweet on Pocahontas. They see each other at church and at Saturday night Bible studies. He also comes by our catechism classes on Sunday afternoons. But it is the simple reading and writing sessions he has with Pocahontas nearly every week that betray his feelings. He likes her, but he knows as a Christian he could not possibly marry her if she did not share his faith as well.

I told Robert—I mean Master Sparkes—what I thought, and he told me to say nothing of this to the Princess. He said, "It is true that Master Rolfe has found a grace and love in his heart extended toward the Princess, but he is very conflicted about it. He would never want her decision about God to be clouded by any other emotion or feeling. He wants her to study the Scriptures, learn about God's love for her, and respond to that first. He is a man of great honor, Elizabeth. He wants nothing more than the best for Princess Pocahontas, and in his mind, the best is for her to find the love of God in her own way."

I assured Robert I would not say anything. Besides, the more Master Rolfe comes to visit Pocahontas, the more likely it is that Robert will come to visit me. Those two seem to go everywhere together. Robert is learning all about tobacco growing from Master Rolfe, and Master Rolfe has called him a very quick learner.

It is Master Rolfe's hope that tobacco will become the crop the colony so desperately needs to make London and the Company take notice of the Virginia colony. So much attention in London has turned to Bermuda where there are no deadly Indians or diseases to deal with. Master Rolfe is afraid that if a valuable crop is not found soon, the stock-holders will cease to care about Virginia.

Elizabeth, what have you heard? Are the stockholders still willing to help us?

Your friend,

Abigail

Rock Hall

October 20, 1613

Dear Elizabeth,

Tonight we had a ball of our own—a harvest ball. The squash and pumpkins have grown large this year. The men have shot a record number of deer and the meat has been stripped, roasted, and salted. There was much merriment in Henricus tonight. We crossed the river to the Citie of Henricus in our boat. The Citie was lit with bonfires (but not too near the thatched roofs!).

Men bowled in the streets. Musicians played flutes and strummed lutes. Everyone sang and danced. Piles of food strained the table boards. Most of it was soon eaten by the merrymakers.

The colonists paid a great deal of attention to Pocahontas, who was dressed in regal fashion. Mrs. Sizemore saw to that. While I dressed in plain linen, Pocahontas stood out in royal blue silk. She looked every inch a princess.

Both Master Sparkes and Master Rolfe were present. Master Rolfe spent most of the evening with Marshal Dale and Governor Gates, but he watched the Princess. He did not dance with her once. Fortunately for me, Robert—I mean Master Sparkes—did not need to worry about appearances.

He danced the night away with me. I had a glorious time. I suppose the dancing shoes your Papa sent for my birthday were not so silly after all.

When we arrived home at Rock Hall, we were tired, but not sleepy. Mrs. Sizemore clucked about us needing our beauty sleep, but we wanted to stay up. Reverend Whitaker found and heated apple cider. We had a mug of the warm drink and talked and laughed about the evening. Reverend Whitaker seemed pleased that Pocahontas had such a good time. He then excused himself and left just the two of us by the fire with our mugs of cider. Pocahontas looked at me. I looked at the fire. I always tried to avoid being alone with her since the day she asked me why I didn't like her.

We were quiet for a few minutes. There was no sound but the crackling of the fire in the fireplace. Pocahontas stared at me. I knew the question she was going to ask before she asked it. "Abigail, you must tell me now. Why do you not like me?"

Yes. It was time. Seeing all that food tonight had made me think of another fall when there was no corn, no food, and no hope.

"Pocahontas, your father is Chief Powhatan, the head of all the Indian tribes in this area. He has much power. He can use it for good or for evil. Four years ago, I lived in James Towne with my father and mother. We came over on a ship from England to start a new life here in America. That year there was very little food. Your people would not trade with the English settlers. Your people kept the corn to themselves and would not help us. Your people watched and waited until we were so hungry we came out of the fort to fish or hunt or gather food. Then they would shoot us with arrows."

Pocahontas sat quietly and listened intently. I continued, "Each of us had a small ration of corn each day. My mother was very sick. I did not know it for a long time, but she would put part of her ration in with mine every day. Soon she was starving to death. Her body got weaker and weaker. Father felt he had to do something. So he went out at night to forage for berries or root vegetables—anything to help Mother. One night he was shot to death by an Indian arrow. Mother lost consciousness and died a few days later, never knowing that Father had died before her."

We sat very still for a long time. I had simply told the facts of what had happened four years before. Finally, Princess Pocahontas stood and said, "Abigail, thank you. Now I understand." She went up the stairs to her bedroom.

I stayed in my chair and stared at the fire while the embers died down. The tears that had been pent up for so long began to flow, and I did not try to stop them. It felt so good to cry, Elizabeth. The pain of the hatred I have carried in my heart seemed to pour out as well. I cried until tears came no more, and then I, too, went to bed.

Your tired friend,

Abigail

London, England

October 30, 1613

Dear Abigail,

I wish you had been with us yesterday. The Lord Mayor was formally installed in a grand show! Never has there been this much pageantry in all the years I have been going. Papa says it is because a well-known playwright wrote and directed this show. It was called *The Triumphs of Truth*.

Early yesterday morning, the newly elected Lord Mayor, the aldermen of the city, and the members of the mayor's company boarded barges for a procession down the River Thames to Westminster Abbey. Because of Papa's friendship with the Right Honorable Lord Mayor, we were able to ride on one of the barges all the way to Westminster. It was a glorious day. The Lord Mayor took the oath, and then we returned on the river to Baynard's Castle landing. All along the way were splendid scenes. They had been erected on river barges by the guildsmen.

Each barge celebrated a different trade. You can imagine the competition among the guildsmen, each determined to demonstrate that their trade is better than the others! They have been working on the barges for months. At the landing, the Lord Mayor was greeted by guildsmen who shouted their cheers for him. He then mounted a triumphal chariot (just like Rome years ago) and rode through the streets to Guildhall. We followed him and saw many pageants along the way and, of course, heard many speeches. After each pageant, the pageant wagons joined in the procession. I think every tradesman in London was part of the spectacle.

At Guildhall, the mayor hosted a banquet for the aldermen, sheriffs, and guild officers. We could not attend this banquet, but there was great merriment in the streets and many vendors of sweets and meats. We had a glorious time.

The bells pealed throughout the day. My favorite show of all was that of Robin Hood and his green huntsmen with their bows and arrows because they let John be one of the Merry Men. He proudly carried the Indian bow you sent him! After the show, torches were lit to escort the Lord Mayor to his home.

There is much more to tell, but Papa says I must hurry and finish. Another ship leaves soon for America, and he wants to put my letters in the barrel he is sending to you. Mother gave much attention to filling this barrel for you. Each October she thinks of your birthday and how your dear mother would have made it special. She has packed many surprises inside the barrel for you.

I will not spoil the surprise in case you read this letter before you open your packages.

Your faithful friend,

Elizabeth

Rock Hall

October 30, 1613

Dear Elizabeth,

Today we had another handwriting class with Reverend Whitaker. He had us copy the Lord's Prayer over and over again until we had a perfect copy. Our hands were sore, and our quill pens were no longer sharp enough to write. Thankfully, we were excused this afternoon. We went straight to the garden to gather pumpkins and squash. There is such a grand harvest this year, and there are still pumpkins on the vine to pick.

Today I showed Pocahontas how to bake a squash pie. We chopped up the squash and a few onions, added some ginger, and then piled the mixture into the pastry. We put the pie pans in the oven under Mrs. Sizemore's watchful eye. It was too glorious a day to stay inside any longer so we begged Mrs. Sizemore to watch our pies for us and take them out of the oven when they were ready. We whipped off our aprons and ran down to the barn to saddle up Admiral for a long ride. The leaves are golden and red and the warmth of the sun is just right for this time of year.

We stopped along a stream for Admiral to get a drink of water. Pocahontas jumped off Admiral's back and ran to the stream. She watched the otters playing and made high-pitched screeching noises that sounded like those the otters made. I laughed, but it made the otters sit up and take notice. A few of them came closer to Pocahontas.

I tied Admiral to a tree and sat down beside Pocahontas. Robert Sparkes had told me a story about the Princesss that I could not believe was true, so I decided to ask her myself. "Master Sparkes tells me you have saved the English from certain death more than once. He said that you even offered your life for John Smith's. Is that true?"

Pocahontas smiled. "John Smith was a good man. He was my elder brother."

I looked at her strangely. "Your elder brother?" I repeated.

"Many years ago, Captain John Smith was captured by my people. The tribe prepared a grand feast to celebrate the execution of the captive English warrior that night. After the feast, two warriors in our tribe brought two large stones before my father, Chief Powhatan. They took them over to Captain Smith and forced his head down on the two stones. The mighty warriors raised their clubs to smash his head.

"I ran over to him and put my body between Captain Smith and the Powhatan warriors. I placed my head on his. If anyone would die that night, it would be me, not Captain John Smith.

"My father, the great Chief, was surprised, for it is only once in my life as a princess that I am permitted to make this sacrifice. Why I chose to do it then for this English warrior, he could not understand. But it was done. Chief Powhatan spared the life of John Smith, and he was adopted into our tribe. Because I gave my life for his, he became my elder brother."

Elizabeth, I had no idea that Pocahontas had done this for Captain Smith. She was only ten years old at the time. How could someone so young be so brave and resourceful?

Pocahontas continued, "Captain John Smith was always very kind to me. I did not want to see the English die. For many months before this happened, I had been carrying baskets of food to the colonists. When I was captured and brought to James Towne, I saw Sam Collier, all grown up now too. He and I used to spin cartwheels together through the streets of the town."

The silence hung heavy. Finally, I asked, "If you brought the English corn in 1607, why didn't you bring it again two years later when the colonists were starving?"

Pocahontas chose her words carefully. "There was a terrible drought that summer. The corn did not grow as we had hoped. Many stalks of corn did not get higher than a few feet. We knew that we had very little supply for our people and none to share. Corn and roots were rationed. Even good spring water was scarce. Many in my tribe died as well.

"But mostly, Abigail, I was afraid of my father. He gave me strict orders not to help the English anymore. Earlier in the very year of which you speak, I learned from my father that he was planning to invite Captain John Smith and his company to a banquet, but afterward he planned to kill them all. I warned Captain Smith of the plot to kill him and his men. I did not know then whether to return home or move on because defying my father would mean the end of my relationship with him. He would rightly question whether my loyalty fell to him or the English.

"The truth was that my loyalty was to Captain Smith. When he was severely wounded and sent back to England to die, I did not know what to do. I had committed an act of treason. Though we never spoke of it, my father knew that I had warned Captain Smith. I did not dare cross him again. What good would it do, anyway? We would not have had enough food for all the English—more than 500 of you—in the year of the drought.

"Captain Smith knew how to negotiate with some of the other tribes. The men left in charge after his deathly wound did not. They only made things worse. I knew no one I could have spoken with that I could trust. Not like Captain Smith."

"My father would have been one you could have trusted," I told her.

Pocahontas replied gently, "Yes, perhaps if I had known him. Perhaps if he were like you. But I knew no one else. My friend, my elder brother, was gone. I had chosen the English with my actions, first in saving Captain Smith and then in warning him. Now that he was gone, I had to choose my Father. He would not have hesitated to banish me from his sight if I had disobeyed. He no longer trusted me and had his warriors keep a close watch on me at all times. He let it be known to all that if I made contact with the English, then I would be executed.

"I do not agree with my father, Abigail," Pocahontas said to me. "I want there to be peace between our peoples. Both of our peoples have killed those who are innocent. Your mother and father. My aunt and her children. This awful war between us must stop, but it cannot as long as we are suspicious of each other."

"I suppose you think you and I should be friends—for the good of our two peoples," I said. I was angry at the thought.

"It would be a start," replied Pocahontas.

Pocahontas gave me much to think about as we rode home. Home. Come to think of it we are both away from what home used to mean to us. We are now both, through no choice of our own, at a home called Rock Hall across the river from Henricus and miles from James Towne. This is home now. Home without mother or father. Home without choice. Home nonetheless.

Never was I so glad to see Reverend Whitaker and Mrs. Sizemore. Even her clucking did not bother me, as she proudly placed our squash pie on the table board for supper.

Much to think about, dear Elizabeth.

Your friend,

Abigail

Rock Hall

November 5, 1613

Dear Elizabeth,

When will another ship come? I very much want to hear from you. We continue in our lessons faithfully each day. I asked Pocahontas why she does not let Reverend Whitaker and Master Rolfe know she speaks, reads, and writes English much better than they think she does. She previously told me she began to learn to read and write English words with Captain Smith years ago. He had written down many words in her language and shown her how to write the English word as well. Pocahontas says that Reverend Whitaker and Master Rolfe both get such pleasure from her every accomplishment, she cannot deny them that joy. She showed me how Reverend Whitaker's face lights up when he realizes she has understood a new idea. I laughed at her impression of Reverend Whitaker. He does so love it when we understand his teaching.

Then, Elizabeth, Pocahontas said something rather strange. "Actually, Abigail, I need time to think and consider this God of yours. It confuses me. I need time for my spirit to understand what my mind is learning. If I slow down the 'mind' learning, then the 'spirit' learning can keep up. I am giving much thought to the things Reverend Whitaker is teaching us. They tug at my heart."

I was shocked. Pocahontas said they tugged at her heart. That is what happens to me too, but I know what it is. It is the Holy Spirit urging me to the truth. Sometimes I don't want to pay attention, but I know that is what it is. I wonder if the Holy Spirit is at work in Pocahontas's heart now to urge her to the truth.

I have to close now. It is my duty tonight to take some feed to Admiral. I have let it get much too late so that I could finish my letter to you. I must hurry or Reverend Whitaker will be cross with me.

I'll write some more tomorrow.

Your friend,

Abigail

Rock Hall

November 10, 1613

Dear Elizabeth,

Much has happened but I have not been able to write until now. After I finished my letter to you nearly a week ago now, I put down my quill. I just had on my shift and prepared for bed. I took my candle to the fire to light it and, holding it aloft in my hand, I made my way to the barn. It was very cold, but I knew I would only be there for a few minutes so I didn't wear my jacket. I put the candle on the niche in the wall of the barn. Admiral was acting very skittish. I told him, "Whoa, boy. It's okay. It's just me, Abigail, with some food."

His ears were back and his eyes were ablaze. Then I saw what he saw—a snake coiled in the hay very near to me. I didn't move a muscle while I tried to think of what to do. Admiral began to neigh louder and become more frightened. I tried to calm him down, but all the time my heart was pounding. I had one eye on Admiral and the other on the snake. "Whoa, boy," I kept saying over and over and tried to reach for his halter to put over his head so that I could lead him out of the stall. Then Admiral reared up and pawed at the stall and me! I was so surprised I didn't notice that he had knocked down the candle into the hay. The hay on the floor of the barn caught fire and just then the snake decided to strike. It bit my ankle! Oh, Elizabeth, be glad there are no snakes in London. It hurt so much as the poison began to spread. The snake slithered away, but I began to feel faint.

I had to get out of the barn, but I couldn't leave Admiral. There are only six horses in the entire colony, and we couldn't lose Admiral. I limped over to Admiral to try to get the halter on him again. He was even more skittish now that the flames were starting to lick the sides of his stall. He railed up again and this time, he knocked me down. My head hit the gate to his stall, and I fell to the ground.

All would have been lost but for Pocahontas. She heard the terrified whinnies of Admiral and knew immediately that something was wrong. She raced down the stairs and out to the barn. Despite the flames, she rushed into the barn, grabbed Admiral's halter, and quickly put it on him. She picked me up and somehow got me on Admiral's back. Then she jumped on his back as well. Pocahontas rode Admiral through the flames into the yard. By that time, Reverend Whitaker and Mrs. Sizemore had rushed outside as well. The three of them watched as the barn burned to the ground in a matter of minutes.

Reverend Whitaker carried me inside and gently placed me on my bed. That was when Mrs. Sizemore saw my ankle. It was burning red to the touch and puffed out twice the size. She knew it was a snakebite and looked with alarm at

Reverend Whitaker. A poisonous snakebite could kill a person in just a few hours.

Pocahontas said, "I know what to do." Relieved, they stepped aside but were shocked when she returned from the kitchen with a knife and cut open the bite wound. Over and over, she sucked the venom from the wound and spit it on the floor. Mrs. Sizemore nearly fainted. If it hadn't been for Pocahontas's quick work, the poison would have spread to my heart and killed me.

I owe my life to the girl I had determined from the beginning to hate.

Your very glad to
be alive friend,

Abigail

Rock Hall

November 12, 1613

Dear Elizabeth,

Reverend Whitaker has been teaching Pocahontas her lessons alone while I recover. Mrs. Sizemore keeps my snakebite wound covered in lemon balm that is prescribed in *The Herbal*. Pocahontas says it is a good thing Mistress Pierce taught me to garden, for my dried herbs are exactly what I need to pull the venomous poison from the wound. Mrs. Sizemore fusses over me, clucking as she goes, but I must admit that I am thankful for her attentions. Pocahontas and I cannot stop laughing when we remember the look on Mrs. Sizemore's face when she saw Pocahontas spitting on the floor. So much for lessons for the royal princess!

After her lessons, Pocahontas visits me, and we talk about what she has learned from Reverend Whitaker. Today, they talked about the need for a sacrifice to pay the penalty of sin. It caused Pocahontas great distress, and I asked her why. I was horrified to find out that her people sacrifice children to Okee, their devil god. If there is a big storm, a long drought, or a long sickness, the priests call for the sacrifice of a child to appease this devil god. Can you imagine, Elizabeth? They believe that if they kill a child, this devil god will go away and leave them alone for a while. The awful thing is that he is never satisfied. Can you imagine growing up wondering if you would be the next child sacrificed to the devil god?

I tried to explain to Pocahontas what Christians believe. Yes, it is true that God said there must be a sacrifice of life to deal with sin once and for all. The difference is that God came here to live here among us. God let Jesus take on the penalty of our sins and be killed in our place. The sacrifice required by God was fulfilled by God. Only a pure sacrifice—God's only son who never sinned—could be sufficient to deal with the penalty of sin once and for all.

Pocahontas asked if there were ever any more sacrifices after Jesus died. "No, because there was no need." She seemed puzzled so I explained, "When Jesus died, God did not leave him in the grave. He resurrected him—made him live again—three days later. Then, God told us that the only requirement after what Jesus did—dying in our place—was to believe that he did this as a way for us to be right with God."

Pocahontas said, "Reverend Whitaker said that God redeemed me with this sacrifice."

"That's right," I agreed. "Just like you redeemed Captain Smith's life with the offering of your own that night, God has redeemed your life with the offering of his own life—his own son's life. That was the last needed child sacrifice, Poca-hontas. God sacrificing his own son because he loves you and me so much."

"But all I have to do is believe this? No more sacrifice?"

I told her that I know it seems strange, but this is exactly what Reverend Whitaker means when he says we are saved by grace. It means we are saved because of what God does, not because of what we do. "When you saved Captain Smith, was it because of anything he did? Was Chief Powhatan going to change his order to kill Captain Smith because of anything Captain Smith did? No, it was because the Chief was pleased with your sacrifice. You offered your life for Captain Smith's and that sacrifice redeemed his life. Now imagine that what you did was done for every man, woman, and child for all of time in one act. Jesus offered up his life as a sacrifice. We know God was pleased with that sacrifice, because he raised Jesus from the dead. He is now our elder brother, Pocahontas, if we will accept what he did to redeem us.

"I know this may sound strange, Pocahontas, but what if Captain Smith had not chosen to let you redeem him from your father's wrath. What if instead of lying there quietly as you placed your body over his and your head between his and the clubs, Captain Smith had gotten up to try to fight for his own life. What do you think would have happened?"

"Why, he would surely have been killed," Pocahontas said.

"That's what I mean by accepting what Jesus has already done for you, Pocahontas. You can fight to please God on your own or trust in the Redeemer's work for you."

"There is so much to think about, Abigail Matthews. Yet what you say does make some sense to me. Something continues to tug on my heart, Abigail, and I will not rest until I fully understand. I am so glad I have you to talk to and that you understand."

Elizabeth, you and Reverend Whitaker are right. I had such a bitterness of soul over the loss of my parents, I could not see what God wanted to do right here at Rock Hall. He let a special person come to live here so she could learn about him. I was so angry at what happened to my parents that I almost missed the chance to be her friend. She thinks deeply, Elizabeth. If she decides to accept the sacrifice of Jesus, it will be with all her heart, her soul, her mind, and her spirit. She does not make this decision lightly. I think she realizes that this will further keep her from being with her father ever again. We must pray for her.

Your snake-bitten,
but very happy friend,

Abigail

Rock Hall

November 23, 1613

Dear Elizabeth,

Master Rolfe visits Rock Hall at least twice a week now. This, of course, is in addition to our daily church services, our Sunday afternoon catechism class, and Marshal Dale's Saturday evening teachings. Robert joins him as often as possible. Robert has asked Reverend Whitaker if he might court me, to which Reverend Whitaker gave a resounding no—at least not until I am seventeen, he added with a wink.

Today both gentlemen stayed for dinner and for a long game of Nine Pins Morris. It was great fun. Pocahontas is very mischievous. She knew that all three men, Master Rolfe, Master Sparkes, and Reverend Whitaker, love their English education and prefer to think of themselves as university men. Pocahontas created a play for them on the education of women in the colony of Virginia. She borrowed Reverend Whitaker's reading spectacles and perched them on her nose. She then read from the Bible with her loudest voice as if she were preaching from the pulpit at the church. She called on each of the men with questions about the Bible passage she had just read, but she wouldn't let any of them answer before she was on to her next question. She had us all laughing at her portrayal of Reverend Whitaker. He laughed the hardest of all. "I suppose I do get rather excited about the teaching of the Scriptures, do I not, girls?"

As Pocahontas gave him back his reading glasses and his Bible, she said, "No better teacher have I had, Reverend Whitaker. A man who loves his God should be the one who teaches about his God to those who do not yet know him." I saw Reverend Whitaker look at her with a glimmer of hope.

It was late in the night before the gentlemen left and Reverend Whitaker retired to his bedchamber. I stayed in Pocahontas's room for a while, and we talked about Robert and John. At least, that is what we call them when we are alone. Pocahontas thinks John is a strong man who works as hard as any Indian warrior she has known. John is nearly ten years older than Pocahontas. Pocahontas says that by the time men are John's age, they realize their limitations as well as their talents and are much easier to live with. We laughed as if we were two schoolgirls sharing secrets. Of course, we are!

Good night, dear Elizabeth. I wish you could meet Pocahontas. You would like her very much.

Your friend,

Abigail

Rock Hall

December 18, 1613

Dear Elizabeth,

Such joy! Not only did I just receive your letters but also the barrel. Your family's generosity again overwhelms me. Please share this letter with your dear Papa and Mother.

Mrs. Sizemore was overjoyed with the quince preserves and the rose-petal potpourri you sent to her. She also thanks you for the herbs. These only grow in England and have such important medicinal uses. After my snakebite, Mrs. Sizemore has been storing up every kind of medicinal herb she can find. Soon she is going to make the hospital planned for Mount Malady totally unnecessary. The sick can just come to Rock Hall.

Reverend Whitaker thanks you and your family for the most recently published *Book of Common Prayer.* He says it is such a thoughtful gift.

I was thrilled with my birthday gifts. Your father continues to send such extravagant gifts to me. The gold chain for me to put Mother's wedding band on and slip around my neck means so much. I have been worried about losing the ring, and it is all I have left of Mother. Please hug your Papa for me. Did you purchase it at the Royal Exchange? It is so lovely and strong, and I will wear Mother's ring close to my heart all the days of my life. Please thank your dear mother for the cookbook, but what I could not believe and am so thankful for is the gift of sugar and spices! Oh, Elizabeth, I will have gingerbread this Christmas. It has been so long, and I was so disappointed that Mrs. Sizemore used up our spices for the gingerbread served when Pocahontas first arrived. Never does a shipment come to me that your mother is not thinking of my most important needs. Again, she sends paper, ink, and seeds. Please thank her for such a variety of seeds. I cannot wait until spring and planting season. Perhaps Mistress Pierce will consider me a rival yet!

Thank you! Thank you! Thank you! My only regret is that this ship will return to you with my letters and my presents for Christmas to your family much after Christmas has passed. Oh, one day wouldn't it be wonderful if our letters could simply fly over the ocean to each other?

Your contented friend,

Abigail

Rock Hall

Christmas Day, 1613

Dearest Elizabeth,

A Merry Christmas to you, dear friend, and to your dear family. Soon the supply ship will bring you my gifts. There is a special chess set for John that Robert helped me make. I have beautiful glass bead necklaces for you and your mother that I made from beads made by the glassblowers in James Towne a few years ago. Tell John that Captain Smith used the beads to trade with the Indians. For your Papa, I have the grandest gift of all. I have given him a framed copy of the Lord's Prayer in my very best handwriting. There. Now he will know his urging of my lessons has not been in vain.

Mrs. Sizemore is having a large crowd of people here today for Christmas dinner. Governor Gates, who will leave in a few months for England, Marshal Dale, Master John Rolfe, Master Robert Sparkes, and alas, many of the church ladies are all to arrive shortly for dinner. I have made gingerbread to share with them, thanks to your dear mother!

We had a wonderful church service this morning. Reverend Whitaker spoke tenderly of the love of God who would willingly send his son to earth in the form of a little baby—not a strong warrior—to win the world to himself through the power of his love for each of us. Pocahontas looked beautiful today as she listened to his words. I feel privileged to know that she is thinking so deeply about all Reverend Whitaker has taught her. If she decides to become a Christian, it will be of her own free will. Anyway, who could make Pocahontas do anything? She is very strong willed.

I must go now and help Mrs. Sizemore with the meal. It promises to be a feast. Please give my love to your father and mother and that dear brother of yours. Tell him I live with a real live Indian and we go to school together. That should impress his friends.

Your friend,

Abigail

Rock Hall

January 16, 1614

Dear Elizabeth,

We do not expect to see John or Robert here this week as the snowdrifts are several feet high. I milked the cows this morning and churned the butter. This is not a task I like to do, but Mrs. Sizemore has not been feeling well. I miss her directing my every move. Today, I made her some pottage. She was very appreciative. She told me I will make a fine wife one day and then surprised me by asking about Master Sparkes. Mrs. Sizemore had a twinkle in her eye. "It is time to consider the attentions of the young man, Abigail. You are nearly seventeen." Nearly seventeen? Why, that is ten months away! I am not ready to be courted, much less married!

"I like Master Sparkes," I told her, "but he is so self-assured and impressed with himself."

"It takes a lot of courage to come to a new world, Abigail. Do not begrudge the young man his bold talk as he may just be bolstering up a fearsome spirit of his own." It was a good thought from a very unexpected source. I think I will talk with Mrs. Sizemore again about this.

Your friend,

Abigail

Rock Hall

January 20, 1614

Dear Elizabeth,

The ground is still covered with snow. Daily church services have been suspended as it is now impossible to get across the river. Reverend Whitaker, always dutiful, rides Admiral to visit the families and the plantations. Tonight he brought back word to us from Master Rolfe that his tobacco was somewhat well received in London, but the quality still does not rival the tobacco from the West Indies. Pocahontas sniffed at that thought and said, "Wait until they taste the tobacco that has been curing since this fall. Then they will see that Master Rolfe's tobacco is the best in the world." "Hmmm," said Reverend Whitaker. " I see you are a big fan of Master Rolfe." Pocahontas quickly retorted, "Well, it was I who told him when to harvest this crop, so I will take full credit if it is the world's finest tobacco yet."

Reverend Whitaker is pleased with how well Pocahontas has learned the basics of our Christian faith. Not only can she say and write the Lord's Prayer and the Ten Commandments but also really seems to understand what they mean. This past month, he has been teaching us about the Apostles'

Creed. He takes each section of the creed and then finds Bible scriptures that explain what the creed means.

Pocahontas told me her favorite part of the catechism is where we say the Creed, then Reverend Whitaker asks: "What dost thou chiefly learn in these Articles of thy Belief?"

Pocahontas and I answer together: "First, I learn to believe in God the Father, who hath made me and all the world. Secondly, in God the Son, who hath redeemed me and all mankind. Thirdly, in God the Holy Ghost, who sanctifieth me and all the elect people of God.

"Her favorite part is about the Son who has redeemed her and all mankind. That, she says, is amazing. No more child sacrifices. No more fear of God. His Son is now her elder brother. This thought brings her much comfort as she ponders the ways of this English God and whether or not to put her trust in him. She told me that if it is true that God redeems her, then she is adopted into his family, and we are then sisters!"

I am so glad that the Lord has dealt with my bitter, angry heart. Pocahontas is a good friend. She and I are very different and yet very much the same. You would really like her, Elizabeth. I wish the two of us could meet.

Your friend,

Abigail

London, England

February 3, 1614

Dearest Abigail,

Your letters and wonderful Christmas gifts just reached us. John marvels at the chess set, and I marvel that your young Master Sparkes could carve such a beautiful gift. You must write to me more about him. I cannot help noticing that your letters speak of him more often and with greater tenderness. Could it be that you are sweet on him?

Father has arranged for a private tutor to school me in the classics, Latin and literature. I still am not permitted to learn about science, but for now, I will be grateful. I am so hungry for knowledge. And you, dear friend, I hope you had your gingerbread for Christmas. Mother and I wish we could have seen the expression on your face when you opened the spices we sent you. I do wish we could be together again.

I have heard rumors from Papa that Governor Gates is returning to London soon to meet with the Company. I am eager to learn all about what is happening with the colony from Papa. Yet it is your life I am most eager to learn about. Your good letters keep you close to my heart.

Your friend,

Elizabeth

London, England

February 4, 1614

My dear Abigail,

I stayed up until the early hours of the morning to read your letters. A snakebite! You must be careful! Bless Pocahontas for knowing what to do and Mrs. Sizemore for nursing you. Your letters let me know that you and Pocahontas are friends. I am glad. I have been praying for you to find someone there in Virginia who can share your life. I know it is so different from the one I lead. Temperance continues to tell me stories of the ten months she was in Virginia. I am afraid I am not as adventurous as the two of you. I have absolutely no desire to go to the brave New World. It requires a brave new heart, which I do not have. Do you know that Temperance, despite all the horrible tales she tells me, sometimes thinks of returning to Virginia? She has begun to correspond with a young captain there, George Yeardley. I wonder if it is to Virginia or to George she wishes to return.

Abigail, I cannot imagine what it has taken for you to be a friend to Pocahontas. I know just seeing her every day has been a challenge as you remember your dear parents.

Yet, from what you said to me in your letters, it appears she, too, has been orphaned by her father. Perhaps when it comes to desiring to belong to a family, you both have more in common than you think.

I hope you will always think of us as your family, and if you do ever want to return to England, you know that Papa and Mother would gladly take you in. Then we could resume our wonderful life together as best friends. Until then, I will be content with your letters.

Your friend,

Elizabeth

P.S. Papa said to tell you he is proud of you. He keeps your elegant writing of the Lord's Prayer on his desk. He told me to tell you that you will make a fine English woman yet. Ha! If he only knew what I know—climbing trees, racing horses, dirty garden fingers, snakebites, and a great disdain for English recipes (all except for gingerbread, of course!).

Rock Hall

February 6, 1614

Dear Elizabeth,

Governor Gates is returning to England on the *Elizabeth* with Captain Adams and is determined to wrap up this Pocahontas problem before he goes. He met with Marshal Dale again this week and is becoming very angry that Chief Powhatan will not bargain for his daughter. The pawn in the political game is becoming worthless to them. It has been nearly a year, and yet Pocahontas remains a hostage here with not a word from her father. It makes me fearful for her. What will they do with her?

I overheard Reverend Whitaker and Master Rolfe speaking quietly. They, too, are worried. Oh, Elizabeth, what is to become of Pocahontas?

Your worried friend,

Abigail

Rock Hall

February 15, 1614

Dear Elizabeth,

Tonight Master Rolfe and Reverend Whitaker met and spoke in low, hushed voices for several hours. Master Rolfe seemed very agitated. He paced the floor. He knelt and prayed with Reverend Whitaker. I do not know what is troubling him so, but I suspect it has to do with Pocahontas.

There is something in the air, Elizabeth. Something is about to happen. I do not know what it is, and I am frightened, especially for Pocahontas. She was away with the church ladies tonight for more etiquette lessons in the ways of English royalty. After all, she is a princess.

I strained to overhear what Master Rolfe was saying, but I only caught bits and pieces of the conversation. Reverend Whitaker was encouraging Master Rolfe to search his heart and see if his desires were pure. Master Rolfe was gravely concerned that he have the Lord's blessing and that nothing he desires be outside of God's will and plan for himself and the colony. I did overhear them both pray that Pocahontas would come to an understanding of God's mercy and grace.

Master Rolfe seems extremely troubled in his spirit. Reverend Whitaker is a wise and good counselor, though, and should be able to help him.

Elizabeth, all I know is that things are about to change. I can sense it in all the activity. The church ladies have stepped up their English princess lessons for Pocahontas. Reverend Whitaker has increased his lessons in the Scriptures. He told me that Pocahontas certainly knows her catechism, but he wants her to know the Word of God. He said that he wants her to understand as much of the Bible as possible without delay. Without delay? What's the hurry? Could it be that soon Pocahontas will be leaving us? Is this why Master Rolfe is so upset?

Your troubled friend,

Abigail

Rock Hall

Dear Elizabeth,

Master Rolfe came over tonight. Again, he and Reverend Whitaker went to the library to speak quietly. Mrs. Sizemore and Pocahontas are with the other church ladies—more lessons. Reverend Whitaker asked me to serve them a hot drink, and I was happy to do it because I was so curious to learn what is going on. I brought in the leather jugs of steaming tea that I made from the wonderful blend of tea leaves your mother sent to me for Christmas. I added some of the sweets that your mother sent as well. It seemed that this was a very important conversation, and I wanted the refreshments to be of equal importance.

When I took the tray to the library, Reverend Whitaker was reading a very long letter. I recognized the handwriting as Master Rolfe's. When I served Reverend Whitaker, I saw that the letter was addressed to Marshal Dale. Oh no, it must be very serious. What could it say? Master Rolfe looked very pensive and troubled. He sat on the edge of his chair and anxiously waited for Reverend Whitaker to read the letter. I lingered as long as I dared. In fact, I know I was troublesome to Master Rolfe, saying anything that came to mind in order to stay a bit longer. "Might I serve you anything else?" "Is there anything else you need?" "Is your tea hot enough?"

"I think Reverend Whitaker caught on, because he removed his spectacles and said coolly, "Thank you, Abigail. We appreciate your hospitality, but we are fine."

What is so important that Master Rolfe had to put it in writing? Why couldn't he simply speak to Marshal Dale himself? What could Master Rolfe have written that needed Reverend Whitaker's review? Why all the secrecy?

What is going on, Elizabeth? I just know it has to do with Pocahontas, but what?

Your friend,

Abigail

Rock Hall

February 18, 1614

Dear Elizabeth,

Now I am sure something is about to happen. Governor Gates, Marshal Dale, Master Hamor, and Master Rolfe all came to Rock Hall today to meet with Reverend Whitaker. Several times, I overheard the name Powhatan. If they are talking about Chief Powhatan, they are talking about Pocahontas. She has so long been with us that I no longer think of her as a hostage but as my friend. I forget that to these men, she is just a political pawn being used in the struggle to establish a colony for England. Oh, Elizabeth, I fear greatly for my dear friend.

I prepared the noonday meal for the gentlemen. I am afraid I rushed, and it was not my best cooking. Nonetheless, I did not want to miss an opportunity to hear what they were discussing. I lingered over my service, trying to be as quiet as a church mouse so they would forget I was there.

Governor Gates is leaving in a few days for England. He asked Marshal Dale if he would be the deputy governor in his stead. Marshal Dale immediately accepted and thanked the

Governor for placing his trust in him. He said as deputy governor he would make every effort to continue the great legacy established during Governor Gates's governance of our colony. *Oh dear*, I thought, as I placed the food on the sideboard. I know Governor Gates is frustrated that he must return to England before securing the ransom demands he made of Chief Powhatan almost ten months ago.

As I filled their drinking jugs, I heard Master Rolfe whisper to Master Hamor that it is likely that Deputy Governor Dale will force Chief Powhatan's hand and use Pocahontas to do so. When I heard this, I took in such a sharp breath that I am sure the gentlemen took notice. I turned away quickly so they would not see the worry on my face. I tried to fade into the background, but desperately wanted to hear every word. I was fairly sure the men had taken no notice of me, but then Reverend Whitaker looked up. He knows me too well. He stood and came close to me with the pretense of asking that I serve more root vegetables.

Then he leaned forward and whispered sternly in my ear, "Not a word of this to Pocahontas, Abigail."

I continued about my serving duties as quietly as possible. Then I heard Master Rolfe speak to Deputy Governor Dale.

"What, sir, do you think should be done with the Princess Pocahontas?"

Deputy Governor Dale replied, "I would not like to see her returned to her people just yet as she has not yet made a commitment to Christ. It is my earnest hope and prayer that she would know the living God and receive him as her own. Nonetheless, we must do what is for the good of the colony and England. Rest assured, all measures will be taken to determine peace with Chief Powhatan—whether through negotiation and bargaining or battle, if we must."

"It will soon be spring," he continued, "and our soldiers have been drilling and training all winter long. They will be fit for battle, if need be."

Reverend Whitaker added, "Even if Pocahontas leaves us soon, she has had much teaching in the catechism and the Scriptures. She is a very intelligent girl, and I am sure that the Word of God has penetrated her heart, if not her will as yet. But know this, gentlemen, I will not perform any rite of baptism without the full assurance of her commitment of heart, soul, mind, and strength to the Lord Jesus Christ. As much as my heart hungers for her to be fully assured of the truth of Jesus Christ, of his love and saving grace toward her, I will never perform the sacred rite of baptism for political ends." He looked steadily at Deputy Governor Dale and Governor Gates when he said this.

Elizabeth, I was so proud of Reverend Whitaker. I was sure at that moment the Governor and Deputy Governor would have been thrilled if Reverend Whitaker had said he would push up her training in the ways of Christianity and then perform the baptism in the next few weeks. Then they would have been free to use Pocahontas. They would brag about their Indian convert to the English powers that be, without one whit of care for her heart and the Lord's timetable in making himself known to her. Then they would use her as a pawn in their political game and feel all puffed up that they were sending their convert back to her people to Christianize them.

Reverend Whitaker gazed steadily at the two men across from him until finally Governor Gates said, "Why of course, Alexander, we yield to you on matters of religion. Pocahontas will not be baptized until you are assured that she has renounced her gods and accepted the one true God."

Elizabeth, the way he said it gave me chills. I could see that the saving of Pocahontas's soul was quite secondary to the political needs at hand. I also saw how Master Rolfe shot a pleading look at Reverend Whitaker. Master Rolfe is in great torment. He is a valiant colonist, through and through, and he has always been obedient to the authorities over him. Yet, now, I can see in his eyes that he is greatly disturbed. I do think he dearly loves my friend Pocahontas. No wonder he and Reverend Whitaker have had so many meetings lately. They are both concerned about the increased talk of using Pocahontas as a ransom for peace or a challenge for war with the Indians.

I must end now. My candle is getting very low. I will write again soon. Please pray that Pocahontas will be protected.

Fearfully,

Abigail

Rock Hall

February 23, 1614

Dear Elizabeth,

Master Rolfe and Master Sparkes visited today. Mrs. Sizemore and Reverend Whitaker withdrew and gave us time together, something they have rarely done before. Do they know the time is short?

Pocahontas is no fool. As soon as we were alone, she faced Master Rolfe and asked, "John, a decision has been made about me, am I right?"

Master Rolfe and Master Sparkes looked at each other. I was surprised, for I had never before heard Pocahontas call Master Rolfe by his given name. John took Pocahontas by the hand, led her to a chair, and bid her sit down. He then knelt by her chair, looked in her eyes, and said, "I will not keep anything from you, Pocahontas. The leaders are talking about what should be done about your father, Chief Powhatan, and the hostilities between our two peoples. The leaders are frustrated because so much time has passed, and your father has not tried to negotiate for your release. In fact, your father has not even inquired about your well-being."

I saw the look in Pocahontas's eyes—she was fighting back tears. I tried to imagine how she must feel. Her father has abandoned her. She has begun to find true love with John. She has found friends in Reverend Whitaker, Mrs. Sizemore, and me. She has begun to get used to English ways and learned to speak and even read English. She has even begun to know our God. Now all this could be stripped from her, just like the English stripped her Indian life from her last April when she was captured by Captain Argall. I cannot even imagine the pain and confusion she must be feeling.

Master Rolfe continued, "Pocahontas, there is talk about trying to force your father's hand concerning you."

Pocahontas replied, "He will never deal with the English. Not even for me—his own daughter, his Matoaka."

Pocahontas turned her face away from Master Rolfe, pondered what he had said, and continued, "Ever since I was a young girl and knew Captain Smith, I found the English a challenging sort. Stupid at times, but not evil. I felt we could find a way to live together. The English have killed so many of my people, and my people have killed so many of the English." Pocahontas stopped when she said this and looked deep into my eyes as I stood near Master Sparkes. "There has been great pain and many sacrifices on both sides."

Then Pocahontas stood up and began to pace the room. "No more!" she said. "John, this must stop!"

Master Rolfe asked, "But Pocahontas, what can we do?"

"I don't know, but there must be a way for both the English and my people to live together in peace."

Master Sparkes stepped forward and said, "John, it is likely the leaders will send an emissary to Chief Powhatan to present the arrangement that Deputy Governor Dale decides upon. Why don't we volunteer? If anyone can speak to the ability of the English to get along with the Indians, it is you. And I will accompany you."

Pocahontas brightened. "Yes, John, you can tell my father about me. He may listen to you. You could explain about my good treatment at the hands of the English and my heart's desire that we all find a path to peace."

I asked, "Isn't that dangerous? Might not Robert and John be killed if the Indians think the English are there to trick or hurt them? After all, it was the English who tricked you into coming onto the *Treasurer* and then abducted you." I blushed when I realized I had called Master Sparkes by his given name, but he was so intensely thinking about this new plan that I do not think he noticed.

John quickly answered, "I will take that risk."

Robert added, "I, as well."

Pocahontas smiled broadly. "Then it is settled."

John and Robert decided to speak with Reverend Whitaker and seek his counsel concerning the idea. Pocahontas and I sat on the steps outside the library straining to hear every word. We could hear very little, but I did hear John Rolfe's voice filled with passion and Reverend Whitaker's steady voice asking questions. Finally, after what seemed to be an eternity, they opened the door.

Reverend Whitaker laughed as he saw the two of us huddled together on the steps so close to the door. "My, my, girls, what have we here? Should we fill you in or have you heard every word already?"

We rushed into the library and said, "Do, please, tell us!"

Reverend Whitaker explained that he thought the plan was sound and that it might lead to a peace that requires no more fighting between our two peoples. Pocahontas sighed with relief and asked if he thought Deputy Governor Dale would approve. Reverend Whitaker then explained the plan in more detail than had John or Robert. It had virtually been settled that in a fortnight Deputy Governor Dale and at least 150 men would sail up to Matchkot, where Chief Powhatan currently resides. They would seek to seal an agreement for the return of Pocahontas or begin the war with the tribes.

Pocahontas exclaimed, "Oh, no!"

Reverend Whitaker said, "You must take courage, dear Pocahontas. God loves you and your people very much. He knows what is in your heart—what he has placed in your heart from your youth. He knows your desire for peace with the English and an end to all the killing. He will not forsake you. Take heart."

I watched Pocahontas's face. She seemed deeply affected in a way I had not seen as she pondered what Reverend Whitaker had said.

"Master Rolfe, Master Sparkes, and I will travel to Deputy Governor Dale's home to discuss this plan with him.

Pray, girls. Pray that he sees the wisdom in this plan. Pray for peace." Pocahontas and I stood with our arms around each other and waved to the men. Mrs. Sizemore came in with two mugs of steaming tea and gave us both a hug.

I suppose she knows more than we thought she did. No wonder the church ladies have been stepping up the pace of Pocahontas's English lady lessons.

As we got ready for bed, Pocahontas asked me, "Do you think I can do as Reverend Whitaker asked? May I pray to the English God? I have not yet decided, Abigail, if I will renounce Ahone and Okee. Will your God hear me?"

"Of course. He wants you to pray to and have fellowship with him. He wants you to know his heart toward you, dear friend. Would you like to pray with me?"

Then, Elizabeth, as we knelt down by the bed in my room, I had the privilege of hearing a pure heart poured out before a loving God. I sense that Pocahontas is ready to receive the gift of salvation from our heavenly Father. She will make her decision in time.

Your exhausted,
but encouraged friend,

Abigail

Rock Hall

February 26, 1614

Dear Elizabeth,

It is settled. Reverend Whitaker told us at our noonday meal that Deputy Governor Dale has agreed. Master Rolfe and Master Sparkes will be the emissaries to Chief Powhatan. The soldiers across the river at Henricus drill daily. Here at Coxendale, other men are drilling as well. It is strange to hear the sounds of war when peace is what is on our hearts.

Robert told me that Deputy Governor Dale is determined to win—one way or the other. It causes me grave concern. Will Robert and Master Rolfe be caught up in the battle? Will they return to us?

Your friend,

Abigail

Rock Hall

March 1, 1614

Dear Elizabeth,

Today a strange thing happened. Pocahontas has been very quiet this last week. She has asked me to read to her often from the Bible. I have heard her practicing the catechism in the quiet of her room. She has refused visits from Master Rolfe and has kept much to herself. Today, she asked Reverend Whitaker if she might speak with him in private. They spent much of the day in the library with the door shut. When they finally came out, Reverend Whitaker had a twinkle in his eye. Of course, I peppered him with questions about what they talked about, but he said simply, "Abigail, you know that some things are kept private."

I asked Pocahontas what she and the Reverend spoke about, and she simply said, "Important matters."

It is not like Pocahontas to be this secretive. Of course, I am dying to know what is going on, but I must respect my friend and be patient. Not exactly my best quality.

Your friend,

Abigail

Rock Hall

March 3, 1614

Dear Elizabeth,

Today Pocahontas asked Reverend Whitaker if she and I could go for a ride on Admiral. Reverend Whitaker had planned to visit Bermuda Nether Hundred and counsel with the parishioners there, but he changed his plans to accommodate Pocahontas's request. Mrs. Sizemore packed us a noonday meal in a basket while Pocahontas saddled Admiral. I hovered around Reverend Whitaker with the hope he would say something—anything—about how Pocahontas was acting. He kept his solemn expression and said nothing.

Pocahontas trotted up from the barn and gave me a hand up onto Admiral's back. We rode a long time and said nothing—both enjoying our freedom. It was an unseasonably warm day and Admiral seemed to enjoy the unrestrained ride as well.

We dismounted near the bank of the James River some distance from the parsonage but still within view of the forts.

We had strict instructions from Reverend Whitaker not to go too far. Somehow, Pocahontas had taken Admiral on a circuitous route, which made it feel like we had been riding forever, even though we were really near where we had started. We spread our meal on a blanket by the river and spoke of many things. She asked about my mother and father and what life was like in England before I came to Virginia. She asked about you and Temperance and my other friends in England. She told me about her brothers and sisters and her mother. She spoke of her father and said she had been hurt by his lack of interest in her rescue.

Then Pocahontas shared with me about her year at Rock Hall. She said, "Abigail, dear Abigail, you really did not like me when I first arrived!"

"Did it show that much?" I asked. We both laughed for we knew that I had been horrible to her. I had let her know in every way possible that I could not stand to be near her.

"Abigail, you were true. I have always known where I stand with you. You do not treat me as a political pawn. You do not treat me as a project—an Indian to be converted or dressed up to become an English princess. You have always, always been absolutely honest with me about what you think." Pocahontas paused for a moment, and then added, "It hurt at times."

"I am sorry for that. I had so much anger and pain in my heart about my mother and father. I took it out on you."

"I know that now."

"Pocahontas, I never in a million years thought you and I would be friends." Again we laughed for we both knew our friendship was an unlikely miracle. I hugged her and added, "Now, we are friends, forever, no matter what happens."

"Abigail, I must ask you something. Please be honest."

"Of course."

"Do you still hate my father?"

I was caught up short. My heart felt pierced.

"Your father? Why do you ask?"

"It was my father who ordered the attack that killed your father. It was my father who ordered the Powhatans to cease trading with the English, which caused your mother to starve to death."

My heart lurched inside me and told me the answer. I knew I must be honest with Pocahontas.

"I have not thought about this for a long time. When the Lord began to work on my heart about my feelings for you, I knew I was taking my pain and anger toward your father and placing it on you. After all, you are the Princess Pocahontas, the daughter of the great Indian chief who destroyed my family. Somehow, though, over time, I was able to separate my feelings for you from my feelings for your father."

"You began to see me as someone different?"

"Yes. Even though I knew in the back of my mind that you are Chief Powhatan's cherished daughter, as they all said in James Towne. I began to think that you were not at all like him. You brought corn to the English for several years. You befriended Captain Smith. You saved Henry Spelman's life. I guess I did see you as different from him."

"If I am returned to my father, I will again be Princess Pocahontas, Princess of the Indian tribe and a servant to my father. I must do his will."

"Must you? Isn't there a higher calling on your life now, Pocahontas? Perhaps the reason you were taken from your people and placed with us for this year is so you could tell the truth about the English—that we aren't all so bad—and that there is a God who loves them so much that he became the final sacrifice for them."

"But if I become my father's daughter, will your hatred for him become hatred for me?"

We remained very quiet. Both of us had asked the other very difficult questions. They were true and strong questions deserving of true and strong answers. We both knew it, and we both knew that to answer then would be to cheapen the questions and trivialize their importance to our lives. We each had an answer to discover—an answer only we could come to in our individual hearts.

We rode silently back to Rock Hall. Admiral seemed to sense our deep thoughts as he plodded slowly back.

Elizabeth, both Pocahontas and I know that the agreement for her return will take place very soon. Our time together at Rock Hall is short, and important questions must be asked and answered. Pocahontas and I may be friends for life, but without these questions settled, we will always wonder how true our friendship really was.

As I prayed tonight, I realized that Pocahontas's question has seared my heart. The Lord has shown me in my heart's response that I do harbor hatred toward the father of the friend my Lord has given me. What will I do with that hatred? It is a troubling, but necessary, question.

Your friend,

Abigail

Rock Hall

March 6, 1614

Dear Elizabeth,

Yesterday I worked alone in my garden. It is there, close to the earth, that I feel closest to God. I took my hoe and turned the soil over and over to prepare it for spring planting. But it was the soil of my heart that was really being plowed by the Spirit of God. The Lord was dealing with me as I worked. Pocahontas's question ran through my mind again and again, but I knew the question behind the question.

Pocahontas knew I had forgiven her. She knew I had worked it all out in my mind. I had mixed up my hatred of her with my hatred of her father and his control over my family's fate. She knew that the ultimate question I had to answer was whether I could forgive her father.

Forgive the man who caused my parents' deaths? Forgive the man who had the power to spare me all this heartache and pain but did not? Forgive the man who has no regrets about what he has done? Just forgive him?

These questions swirled around in my mind. What difference does it make anyway? I am not going to meet him—we could even be at war with him in just a few short weeks. Why is this a question I must consider? What does it matter?

I tugged and tugged at some weeds that had deeper roots than usual. I pressed down hard on my hoe with my foot to try to lift up the roots, but I could not get them to budge. I fell to the ground exhausted. With dirt covering my face and hands, I began to sob uncontrollably. All the years of pain and loneliness came crashing in on me. I have tried to be so brave. I have tried to be thankful for the goodness of God. After all, the Pierces, Reverend Whitaker, and Mrs. Sizemore have all taken very good care of me. And I do appreciate them. Really I do. It's just that there is a terrible ache inside. I can no longer feel the arms of a mother around me or the strong hand of a father on my shoulder. I can no longer remember the sound of their voices.

When I think of all I have lost, a terrible, horrible, agonizing ache presses on my heart.

Did I hate Chief Powhatan? Yes! Yes! I hated him with all my heart. If only he had shown compassion, Mother and Father would be alive today. I pounded the ground with my fist and hurled question after question at God. Why had he allowed this to happen? Couldn't he have stopped Chief Powhatan? Couldn't he have taken only my father or my mother—why did he let both of them die?

I lay in the garden, covered in dirt and mud. My face was wet with tears, my heart heavy and my soul distraught. Not another word came from my mouth. I was finished with my questions. I was so quiet that I should have heard

Reverend Whitaker enter through the garden gate. He sat down beside me and pulled a worn Bible from his jacket. "Abigail," he said very softly, "you are asking important questions. Questions of the heart. Questions of life. There is not a generation that passes that does not face and ask these same questions. Is God really there for you, Abigail? Is he there for you when all life's circumstances seem to shout otherwise? Can you trust him, Abigail? With your mother? Your father? With your own life? You know much about him, Abigail, but do you know him? Can you abandon yourself to him and know he loves you? Can you, in adversity as well as joy, in blessings as well as difficulties, trust your heavenly Father?"

I wrapped my arms around my knees and pulled them up close to my chest. "If I forgive Chief Powhatan, then what do I have left?"

"Ah," answered Reverend Whitaker. "We get to the heart of it finally." Reverend Whitaker was silent for several minutes and then said, "Abigail, are you afraid that if you let go of your anger and hatred of Chief Powhatan that somehow you will disgrace the memory of your own father?"

I began to cry again, but this time the tears were soothing and cleansing. The questions Reverend Whitaker was putting to me now were those that had whirled around in my heart these last four years. But I had been afraid to face them. Somehow, hearing him ask them made them seem less frightening. Yes, it was true, somehow my hatred of Chief Powhatan is keeping the memory of my parents alive. It is as if that is the only way I know to protect them or at least protect their memories.

"Our Lord taught us to forgive, Abigail. How many times in class have you written his own prayer to our heavenly Father? Jesus said, 'Father forgive us our trespasses as we forgive those who trespass against us.' Abigail, Jesus knew we needed God's help to forgive those who hurt us. It is not something you can do on your own. He is here now, Abigail, to help you forgive. Are you able to trust him? Remember what Jesus said, 'Trust in God and trust in me.'

"Abigail, you have known Jesus for many years. He is taking you on a deeper walk with him—asking you to trust him when there are no clear answers. Is not that what trust is really all about? If you could see clearly, you would have no need to trust in him. You are a strong, bright girl, Abigail. This, however, is not so much a matter of the mind as it is a matter of the heart. Here," he said handing me his Bible, "let God speak to you." He gave me a hug and walked quietly away. I sat for a few minutes with the tears still sliding down my face. Before I even opened the Bible, I knelt there in my garden and forgave Chief Powhatan and even God for taking away my parents. The numbness in my heart began to seep away as I opened the Bible to Psalm 40 and read:

I waited patiently for the Lord;
He turned to me and heard my cry.
He lifted me out of the slimy pit, Out of the mud and mire;
He set my feet on a rock
And gave me a firm place to stand.
He put a new song in my mouth, a hymn of praise to our God.
Many will see and fear and put their trust in the LORD.

Suddenly, I knew what I must do. I jumped up and brushed myself off. I tucked Reverend Whitaker's Bible under my arm and ran back to the parsonage. I found Pocahontas in the barn, grooming Admiral.

"Abigail?"

I am sure I looked frightful with my dirty face showing streaks where the tears had been.

"Pocahontas, you were right. I did hate your father. I hated him with all my being—but no more. I did not even realize how much hatred I carried in my heart until the Lord showed me why I could not let it go. It was sin—pure sin— and it was keeping me from trusting him with my life as an orphan. I am so sorry I could not see it before. It must have caused you great pain. Dear friend, will you forgive me for hurting you by carrying so much hatred in my heart toward your father?"

"Forgive you? I do not understand."

"My hatred and anger have been festering inside me for four years. When you came, I did not want to be around you. As I got to know you, I let my anger toward you slip away. But, I kept my anger and hatred toward your father. When I confessed this to God in the garden, I asked him to take away my hatred. He surprised me, though. He told me to lay it down. It was I who took up this hatred, and I was the one who would have to lay it down again. Then he told me to trust him to fill up the holes in my heart. I do, now. I really do. A new song has come in my heart, one I have not heard for a very long time.

"Yet, Pocahontas, I see now how much my sin must have hurt you all this time we have been living here at Rock Hall together.

"You are lonely too. You also miss your father. I would never let you speak of him. I said horrible things about him. I tried to feed your own sadness about how he would not negotiate for you. I wanted you to hurt because of your father as much as I hurt because of him. Princess Pocahontas, daughter of the King of great and mighty tribes, will you forgive me for such horrible, cruel behavior?"

Pocahontas stood there next to Admiral with tears in her eyes. "Yes," she answered. We threw our arms around each other. I have never been so full of joy. We walked back to the parsonage with our arms around each other, happy and content in the knowledge that our friendship was forever.

Your friend,

Abigail

Rock Hall

March 18, 1614

Dear Elizabeth,

Today Master Rolfe and Master Sparkes came to visit. In a few days, they will leave with Deputy Governor Dale and some 150 men to sail to Pamunkey, home of Chief Powhatan, to discuss an arrangement with him. Master Rolfe spent more than an hour alone with Reverend Whitaker. Robert explained to me that John is very much in love with the Princess Pocahontas but dares not express it to Deputy Governor Dale. He has been struggling with his feelings for months and has frequently sought the counsel of Reverend Whitaker, because he knows the Bible would not have him be unequally yoked in marriage with an unbeliever. He had hoped that Pocahontas would become a Christian, but if she will not, he cannot marry her. It has been an agonizing but necessary decision. It must be particularly difficult for him to say good-bye to Pocahontas now. He has never expressed his feelings to her. He has remained a faithful friend to her.

Robert told me that at one point, Master Rolfe spent days writing out his thoughts about the Princess in a letter to Deputy Governor Dale. In the letter, he asked for approval to marry Pocahontas, but he withheld the letter because Pocahontas had not yet decided to become a Christian. Without that decision first, she could never be his wife.

I asked Robert where the letter was now. He told me that he thought Reverend Whitaker was keeping it safe. Robert said that John's love for Pocahontas is very strong and deep, but deeper still is his commitment and love for the Lord. His hopes that she would come to know and receive the Lord Jesus were dashed when all this talk of returning her to Chief Powhatan began. Robert said that Reverend Whitaker was especially moved by John's commitment to Pocahontas. They both agreed that neither would push the question of her salvation because of their own desires to see her become a Christian.

Pocahontas and John Rolfe took a long walk together, while I showed Robert some of my new plants in the garden. When they returned, Reverend Whitaker gathered us in the library with Master Hamor, who had just arrived. Master Hamor told Master Rolfe and Master Sparkes that the plans for the journey are now finalized.

Master Hamor explained that Deputy Governor Dale had several ships ready for the journey to Matchkot. Master Rolfe and Master Sparkes needed to leave now to discuss how to negotiate for Pocahontas's ransom. Pocahontas will be returned to Chief Powhatan if he returns all English weapons, all other prisoners, and provides a ship full of corn. If the negotiations fail, then Deputy Governor Dale is prepared to begin the battle right then and there.

Pocahontas asked, "How will 150 English fare against a thousand of my father's best warriors?" Pocahontas and I looked at each other. We were both afraid for John and Robert.

"The soldiers will be heavily armed and protected by armor."

Master Hamor continued, "Princess Pocahontas, you are to come with us on the ship." We all looked at each other with stunned expressions. "Deputy Governor Dale suspects that your father will not deal unless he knows you are well-treated. He asked me to tell you to ready yourself."

Reverend Whitaker must have read my mind. "Might I recommend that Miss Matthews accompany the Princess? She can tend to her needs."

Master Hamor said thoughtfully, "It might help the negotiations with the Chief if he knows the English have honored his daughter as the Princess she is. Hmm . . . a handmaid might be a good addition to the plan. I will check with Deputy Governor Dale."

After he left, John, Robert, Pocahontas, Reverend Whitaker, and I sat in the library and tried to sip tea and make conversation. Master Hamor said we should expect to sail in three days.

"Reverend Whitaker, I must thank you for your quick thinking to ask about Abigail," said Pocahontas. "She has been a constant companion this last year and a good friend."

No one wanted to talk about the obvious—that none of us may be with Pocahontas again after this week. Then Master Rolfe and Master Sparkes left.

Pocahontas went up to bed. It was just Reverend Whitaker and me sipping our tea.

"John Rolfe loves Pocahontas," I said boldly.

"Yes, I know," he replied.

"Well, what are you going to do about it?"

"What should I do? It is out of my hands."

"No, it isn't. You have in your safekeeping a letter that could change everything."

Reverend Whitaker was startled. "How do you know about the letter?"

"Robert. John must have told him." We were silent for a while and then I said, "Well, I just thought you should know that I know."

Elizabeth, there is not much time now. In a few days, we leave on the *Treasurer*.

Your friend,

Abigail

Rock Hall

March 21, 1614

Dear Elizabeth,

We have not seen Master Rolfe or Master Sparkes for the last few days. They meet daily with Deputy Governor Dale.

Reverend Whitaker prayed for us tonight. Then just as I was leaving to go to my room, he called me back to the library. He gave me a small leather envelope and told me to open it. I did. Inside was a letter several pages long. I saw this was the letter John Rolfe had given to Reverend Whitaker.

"Abigail Matthews, this is now entrusted to your care."

"But Reverend Whitaker, what will I do with it?"

He said, "The Lord will show you what to do with it."

I did not understand what he meant, but I hugged him and hurried to my room to place the leather packet carefully with my belongings.

Your friend,

Abigail

The Treasurer

March 22, 1614

Dear Elizabeth,

How odd to be on this ship, the *Treasurer.* How much stranger still for Pocahontas. She has not been on this ship since Jazapaz, an Indian, sold her for a copper kettle. We are staying in the gunner's cabin, the very room that Pocahontas was locked in when she was abducted. There is no lock on the door now.

Pocahontas has been quiet and reading the Bible. She has asked me several times to read the more difficult passages to her. She spends much time in what appears to me to be prayer. Whether she is praying to Ahone or God, I do not know.

Deputy Governor Dale wants Chief Powhatan to know he means business. He has told the Indians he can come in peace or war, but the choice is Chief Powhatan's.

Your friend,

Abigail

The Treasurer

March 24, 1614

Dear Elizabeth,

What a horrible day! When Deputy Governor Dale again spread the word to the Indians that he comes for peace or war, he got an answer. Showers of arrows came from everywhere and wounded one of his men.

That was all it took. The men went ashore. They burned some 40 houses and took food and other goods, and five or six Indians may have been killed. Deputy Governor Dale knew the message would soon get to Chief Powhatan that he means business. The Chief must deal regarding Pocahontas or war will begin.

Pocahontas is in great distress and remains secluded in the gunner's cabin of the *Treasurer.* I am to be with her at all times. I can tell she is in much agony. I am trying to be very quiet. Sometimes the best thing a friend can do is just be there.

Your friend,

Abigail

The Treasurer

March 26, 1614

Dear Elizabeth,

We have been anchored here at Matchkot, where Chief Powhatan is supposed to be, for two days. But nothing happened. No Indians. No arrows. No sounds. Then we saw the response. Four hundred Indians with bows and arrows stood on the shore. Our men also went ashore protected in armor and well armed. Would anyone fire the first shot? The Indians made no show of fear. They walked up and down among the English and demanded to know where our king was. They wanted to speak to him.

Deputy Governor Dale said that if the Indians attacked, they were ready for war, but asked if they could send a message to Chief Powhatan. Deputy Governor Dale has given them until noon tomorrow. Then the fight will begin. He even promised to give them a warning by trumpet and drum before the attack.

While we were waiting, two brothers of Pocahontas arrived. They very much wanted to meet with their sister to see if she was all right. Master Rolfe and Master Sparkes came to the gunner's cabin to get Pocahontas. I watched as she walked on the riverbank to meet them. Her brothers seemed overjoyed to see her. I could not understand what they were saying, but I could tell they thought she looked well. They talked for a long time.

Pocahontas explained to Deputy Governor Dale that her brothers would send word to her father that she is well, that she should be redeemed by the Chief, and that a peace should be concluded between the two peoples. In exchange for the two brothers coming on board, Master Rolfe and Master Sparkes would be dispatched and taken to Chief Powhatan to conduct the negotiation.

Master Rolfe looked back at Pocahontas, who nodded ever so slightly at him. The look in their eyes spoke volumes, however, and I thought of the letter waiting in the pocket of my jacket in the gunner's cabin. Robert tipped his helmet to me and seemed much more self-assured than I felt, but then I remembered what Mrs. Sizemore had said. I waved to him. Pocahontas and I stared as the two men walked with the Indians into the forest along the shoreline.

For most of the afternoon, Pocahontas and her brothers visited with each other. They spoke in their native language, and I could not understand what was being said. I could tell that they loved each other very much and were glad to be together again.

Later that afternoon, Pocahontas's brothers were given food and treated well. Pocahontas came to find me.

"Abigail, I must tell you some things that you can later share with John—especially if tomorrow I am redeemed by my father. I could not say anything until now. Not long ago, I decided to forsake Ahone and Okee and receive Jesus Christ as my Lord and Savior. I now worship the English God. I asked Reverend Whitaker not to say anything to you or anyone for a long while. I needed to know if this choice I had made would be strong. I needed to know if I would be faithful to God no matter what happened. When I first heard of the plan to attempt peace by negotiating for my return, I struggled with my own desires. I wanted to stay at Rock Hall with you and Reverend Whitaker. And, I wanted to stay with John. Yet, I also thought a great deal about what you had said to me concerning a higher calling. I thought of all that God did to sacrifice his own son's life for me, and I found that I wanted to serve him more than anything—even if it meant I would lose my friends and my new life. Perhaps it is in the returning to my people that peace will finally be made between our two peoples. Perhaps even if I must return, I will be able to tell them about the God who does not require human sacrifice.

"I do not know what will happen tomorrow when John and Robert return, but I know this. I know that God loves me and he loves you. I know he will keep our two hearts bound together in friendship forever. Thank you for showing me the breadth and depth of the forgiveness of God. When you were able to forgive my father, I knew then that your God is able to do wondrous things. I knew then he could even make peace between our two peoples. What I did not know was that this might require me to return to my people. Yet I am willing if that is what he wants for me."

"Oh, Pocahontas, I do not want you to go. You are more than my friend. You are like a sister to me. There must be another way."

"The Lord will watch between me and you, Abigail. He will do what is right."

"Pocahontas, do you know of John's deep love for you?"

"I have suspected it for some time, but I knew he was troubled."

"The Scriptures speak of not being unequally yoked with an unbeliever. He would never have wanted you to know of his love before you had made your own decision about whether or not to believe in Jesus. He spoke with Reverend Whitaker, though."

"John is a good man. Robert, too, Abigail."

"I will miss our talks, Pocahontas."

"Perhaps if there is peace, we can visit again."

We hugged each other, and Pocahontas returned to her brothers. I stayed in the cabin a long time and prayed. Suddenly, I knew what God wanted me to do. I grabbed the leather pouch and sought out Master Hamor.

"Master Hamor, sir, may I have a word with you?"

"Certainly, Miss Matthews, what might I do for you?

"Reverend Whitaker entrusted a special letter to me, and now I will entrust it to you."

He looked at me quizzically, but took the leather packet. He found a quiet spot on the ship, sat down, and opened the packet. I watched his face as he read the letter. I had not read it, but I could guess what it contained. I watched him read it once. Then twice. Then once more. He slowly folded the letter and put it back in the leather packet. Then he put the packet in his jacket pocket and turned to watch the river.

After what seemed like hours, I saw him stride over to Deputy Governor Dale and the two of them went below to the Captain's quarters.

That night Pocahontas and I prayed together. We prayed for John's and Robert's safety. We prayed for God's will. We prayed for peace. We thanked God for each other. I did not say anything about the letter—after all, I really did not know what was in it.

I do not think either Pocahontas or I slept well that night.

Your friend,

Abigail

The Treasurer

March 27, 1614

Dear Elizabeth,

We were so overjoyed to see John and Robert return. Of course, as anxious as we were for the report, they went directly to the Captain's cabin to meet with Deputy Governor Dale and Master Hamor. I wondered if Master Hamor had shown anyone John's letter. I wondered what it said. The men stayed there for more than two hours. Pocahontas and I walked the deck of the ship arm in arm. Words were not necessary as we waited for the news. Had her father redeemed her?

Finally, the men came up on deck for a walk. Deputy Governor Dale told us that the mission had gone well. Chief Powhatan, fearing the tricks of the English, would not meet with Master John Rolfe and Master Robert Sparkes. Instead they met with the Chief's brother Opechankano, who is the next in line for chief. He assured them he would use his influence to further our requests.

Pocahontas asked, "So we do not know whether my father will redeem me?"

Deputy Governor Dale replied, "No. But then, your father may have other decisions to make." He smiled as he walked away.

Pocahontas and I looked at each other. What could he mean?

Then Master Rolfe asked if he could escort Pocahontas on a short walk. He was quite formal. Again, Pocahontas and I looked at each other. The men were acting very strangely. Robert told me of his adventure in the company of the Indians, but I was distracted. I much preferred to know what John and Pocahontas were speaking about. When they returned, Pocahontas was smiling and John winked at Robert. It seemed that I was the only one in the dark.

John said, "I hear I am to thank you, Miss Abigail." I must have looked perplexed for he continued, "I understand a certain letter I wrote and entrusted to Reverend Whitaker found its way to your care."

"I did not read it, John. But I guessed it had to do with your love for Pocahontas."

"A love that would have remained silent if you had not acted as you did. Why did you give the letter to Master Hamor?"

"Robert told me of your noble treatment of Pocahontas and that, despite your feelings for her, you would not tell her until she had made a decision about her faith. You did not want to influence her in any way. What you did not know, John, was that Pocahontas has made a decision to become a Christian. I only learned of it a few nights ago. She, too, did not want her feelings for you to confuse that important decision. I suspected, knowing your deep faith, John, and your many hours of secret conversations with Reverend Whitaker, that you were struggling with whether or not you could ask the Princess to marry you if she chose not to become a Christian."

John laughed and said, "You are a very wise girl."

"It seemed as though all our lives were about to be changed by a decision made by Deputy Governor Dale. I thought that he should know all the facts if he was about to make an important decision about Pocahontas's fate. I had no idea if Master Hamor would give the letter to Deputy Governor Dale, but since you addressed it to him, I suppose I hoped so."

"Ah, and that is exactly what happened. Deputy Governor Dale is elated with the prospect of a marriage between Pocahontas and myself. But first, of course, I had to know whether Pocahontas would be equally as pleased."

"And?" I asked, looking at Pocahontas.

She leaned on John's arm and said, "Abigail, John has told me of his love and his desire for marriage. I would like that, too, but only if it will help bring about the peace we all so desire. I have asked John to go to my father and ask him if he will bless our marriage. If so, I will be delighted to become Mrs. John Rolfe."

Oh, no, Elizabeth, more *waiting!* I can hardly stand it. What if her father says no? What then?

Your friend,

Abigail

The Treasurer

March 28, 1614

Dear Elizabeth,

The waiting is over. John and Robert again went to visit the Chief. This time, accompanied by her brothers, he was willing to hear of John's request to marry his daughter Pocahontas. Robert told me that John passionately pleaded for the hand of Pocahontas in marriage and promised to honor her all her days. It must have been pleasing to Chief Powhatan because he swiftly gave his approval. Back on ship, all were rejoicing as we set sail for Henricus. I can't wait to tell Reverend Whitaker. And Mrs. Sizemore! Oh, my goodness, will she ever be pleased. I can see her now, fiddling with every nip and tuck in a wedding dress for the Princess.

We are all exhausted, but very, very happy.

Your friend,

Abigail

Rock Hall

March 31, 1614

Dear Elizabeth,

Today Reverend Whitaker baptized Pocahontas into the Christian faith. Mrs. Sizemore and the church ladies had spared no effort. The church was decorated with the early spring flowers. The baptismal font was filled with fresh spring water. Reverend Whitaker looked splendid in his white robes. Reverend Bucke from James Towne and many others attended. I was thrilled to see the Pierces again. Jane is growing up fast, a girl of 13 now. She is quite lovely. She asked about you, Elizabeth, as she knows what dear friends we are. She asked that you give her love to Temperance. Temperance was always such a dear to Jane and kept her cheerful during that horrible year with no food.

Princess Pocahontas looked radiant in a white robe that Mrs. Sizemore had sewn. Mrs. Sizemore has been busy with both the baptismal robe and the wedding dress to prepare in less than ten days. The wedding is less than a week away. You can't imagine the clucking going on at Rock Hall these days!

The baptism service was quite remarkable. Reverend Whitaker presented Pocahontas to those in attendance. Having desired to come to holy baptism and having been instructed in the catechism, she was now ready to make her confession of faith and to receive the baptism. He said that she would today receive a new name, the name of Rebecca.

Reverend Whitaker asked Pocahontas—I mean, Rebecca—many questions of the faith. Rebecca renounced the devil and all his works. I could not help but think of the devil god Okee that she had learned to fear—the devil god who demanded child sacrifices. Rebecca spoke the creed in a strong voice, and at the end said, "All this I steadfastly believe."

Reverend Whitaker said, "I baptize thee in the name of the Father, and of the Son, and of the Holy Ghost. Amen." Her face radiant, she looked steadily at Reverend Whitaker, who spoke of what this act of baptism means. Then we all bowed our heads and prayed the Lord's Prayer. Reverend Whitaker turned to Rebecca and said, "As for you, Rebecca, who have now by Baptism put on Christ, it is your part and duty also, being made the child of God and of the light by faith in Jesus Christ, to walk answerably to your Christian calling and to follow the example of our Savior Christ, and to be made like unto him; that as he died and rose again for us, so should we who are baptized die from sin and rise again unto righteousness."

Mrs. Sizemore, who was sitting with me, passed me a handkerchief as I was crying. We both dabbed at our eyes as we realized the incredible miracle that had taken place in

Pocahontas's long journey to faith in Jesus. I stole a glance at Master Rolfe, who gazed upon Rebecca, beautiful in her white robe and shining face, with such joy. That afternoon the streets filled with people. Music filled the air and all made merry as we celebrated the baptism of Pocahontas. When I asked her what she thought of her new name, she said that Reverend Whitaker had chosen it, but had asked her about his choice. He read her the story in the Bible of Isaac, Abraham's son, and Rebekah and the miracle of how they found each other, each trusting in the will of God for their marriage.

John and Rebecca walked together through the crowd. Soon, they will be married. I could not be happier for my friend and companion, dearest Pocahontas, little Snow Feather, who is now Rebecca, which means in English, "to bind closely to another."

Reverend Whitaker came by and whispered in my ear, "God used you to draw Pocahontas to himself."

I looked at him with surprise.

"Do you remember that day in the garden a few days before the *Treasurer* left? Pocahontas had already made her commitment to Jesus more than a month before. Yet, she was not sure that you would approve. She told me she would not make a public declaration of her faith until she was sure it would not hurt you."

"What?"

"She knew that the loss of your mother and father deeply affected you. She was not sure you could share your heavenly Father with her. She thought that if you found out she had become a Christian, you would resent her and think that she had taken away your heavenly Father as well as your earthly father. I tried to tell her this would not be so, but I think, Abigail, she knew more about your pain than I did. I encouraged her to talk with you about it. When she asked if you could forgive her father, she was really wanting to know if you had room in your heart for her to know your heavenly Father and call him her own. She loves you very much and did not want to hurt you.

"When you forgave Chief Powhatan for his role in the death of your parents and when you sought Pocahontas's forgiveness for how you had treated her, she knew the power of the forgiveness of Christ in a way she had not understood before. She responded to it completely."

"I had no idea."

"Usually we don't, Abigail. The power of forgiveness, especially forgiveness that comes at great cost, is a power we likely will never fully understand until we get to heaven. The Scriptures tells us that what is bound on earth is bound in heaven and what is loosed on earth is loosed in heaven. We cannot even imagine the power of the grace of God."

I am deeply humbled. I have learned much in this year with Pocahontas. I've learned much about myself and much about my heavenly Father.

Your friend from Rock Hall
the place of new names,

Abigail

James Towne

April 4, 1614

Dear Elizabeth,

Tomorrow is the wedding! Reverend Bucke and Reverend Whitaker will both perform the ceremony at the church here.

Oh, my, have the church ladies been busy. This past week, I have had to rescue Rebecca from Mrs. Sizemore more than once. She managed to gather the finest Dacca muslin, a veil of lace, and a robe of fine English brocade to make Rebecca's wedding dress. Where do you suppose the robe of fine brocade came from? Your father's birthday gift to me of several years ago has finally found its rightful home.

Rebecca and I are staying with the Pierces. Mistress Pierce is such a no-nonsense woman that we find ourselves right at home. Jane adores Rebecca and has been busy picking flowers to decorate the church. Chief Powhatan sent a beautiful freshwater pearl necklace for his daughter to wear.

He will not attend the wedding, but he sent two of Pocahontas's brothers and her uncle Opitchapan. They brought two baskets of dirt, another present from her father. Chief Powhatan is giving his daughter and John Rolfe many acres of valuable land. The baskets of dirt are from that land. Pocahontas's brothers are having a fine time. They brought venison for the wedding feast. John and Robert are making sure they feel welcome. They have even taught them to bowl.

Tonight, it took all of us to get Mrs. Sizemore to leave. The wedding is in the morning so she brought over the wedding dress, the veil, the robe, and the shoes. She doesn't trust us. She was clucking around quite a bit and seemed reluctant to leave her treasures in our care. Mistress Pierce assured her that Rebecca would be properly dressed and ready long before the ceremony. After repeated assurances that we would not muss the dress, Mrs. Sizemore finally left.

Mistress Pierce, always thoughtful of others, took Jane to visit the Smythes and left us alone. Rebecca and I laughed as we recalled our many adventures of the past year. I gave my impression of her in her first English corset tied tight around her ribs, and she gave her impression of me learning to ride Admiral. We have taught each other much this year, but nothing more important than the value of true friendship. On this last night before her wedding, we agreed we will be friends forever. Rebecca asked if she could have one last special favor—to carry my father's Bible during the wedding ceremony. It brought such joy to me to think that she would honor my father in this way. I wish she had known him, Elizabeth. They would have really liked each other.

With great joy,

Abigail

James Towne

April 5, 1614

Dear Elizabeth,

It is late now, and the Pierces' home is quiet. I have a
few minutes to write to tell you about the wedding. It was all
we could have hoped for. The bells rang this morning at
10:00 a.m. to call everyone to the church. I stayed with
Mistress Pierce and Mrs. Sizemore to help Rebecca get ready.
On the second bells, we walked with Rebecca to the church.
I lifted the end of her robe to keep it from touching the dirt.
Rebecca wore the pearl necklace from her father. She carried
my father's Bible with a bouquet of flowers that Jane had
gathered for her. She looked so beautiful. We took her to her
uncle Opitchapan, who willingly gave her away. Her brothers
stood with him and yet looked tenderly at their sister. They
know she is happy now.

John Rolfe, with Robert Sparkes by his side, could not
take his eyes off his bride as she approached the front of the
church. Reverend Whitaker stood at the front of the church.
He was beaming. What a glorious day for all of us.

After they stated their vows and John placed a ring on
Rebecca's hand, Reverend Whitaker prayed, "O eternal God,

Creator, and Preserver of all mankind, Giver of all spiritual grace, the Author of everlasting life, send thy blessing upon these thy servants, this man and this woman, whom we bless in thy name; so these persons may surely perform and keep the vow and covenant betwixt them made, and may ever remain in perfect love and peace together, and live according to thy laws; through Jesus Christ our Lord."

Reverend Bucke turned to the congregation and said, "Forasmuch as John and Rebecca have consented together in holy wedlock, and have witnessed the same before God and this company, and have given and pledged their troth each to the other, and have declared the same by giving and receiving of a ring, and by joining of hands, I pronounce them to be man and wife together in the name of the Father, and of the Son, and of the Holy Ghost. Amen."

After communion, Reverend Whitaker prayed, "Look, O Lord, mercifully upon them from heaven, and bless them. And send thy blessing upon these thy servants; that they obeying thy will and always being in safety under thy protection, may abide in thy love unto their lives' end; through Jesus Christ our Lord. Amen."

Amen! The bells began to ring and continued until everyone had left the church. Mr. and Mrs. John Rolfe were surrounded by many well-wishers. I was content to watch from afar. There was much feasting and celebration, for not only was this a marriage of deep and abiding love, there was great hope this would be a marriage of peace. Watching Rebecca's brothers and uncle enjoying themselves during the feast made me wonder if this dream might be possible. If anyone could bring peace to this troubled colony, it would be Pocahontas—a girl who always knew her own mind, a strong-spirited, determined girl who for years had dreamed of peace between her people and the English. Perhaps now in this most unusual and unexpected way, there will be peace.

Dear Elizabeth, your father can rest easy now. If anyone can make a go of this colony, it will be John and Rebecca Rolfe, partners in business, and partners of the heart. Robert has asked Reverend Whitaker again if he might court me. Perhaps that is not such a bad idea after all.

Forever your friend,

Abigail

Epilogue

In 1615, Thomas was born to John and Rebecca Rolfe. Chief Powhatan promised that as long as Pocahontas lived there would be peace.

In 1616, the Virginia Company decided England should meet the American Princess, Lady Rebecca. Rebecca traveled to London with her family and her sister Matachanna. Rebecca attended plays, dinners, balls, and pageants. In early 1617, John Rolfe moved his family to the English countryside for a break from the activities and the unhealthy city air of London.

When Rebecca and Thomas fell ill, the Rolfe family set sail for Virginia. When Rebecca took a turn for the worse, they landed at Gravesend for medical help. John carried Rebecca to a cottage near the waterfront. For several days, Rebecca struggled against her illness. Reports noted that she expressed her trust and hope in God and her beloved Savior. She died on March 21, 1617, and was buried the same day in St. George's Parish.

The grieving husband set sail again to Virginia, but Thomas's condition worsened. John Rolfe finally agreed to leave Thomas in the care of his brother rather than risk the loss of his son's life as well. When Thomas was old enough to survive the difficult conditions of Virginia, he would be reunited with his father. Unfortunately, John Rolfe died when Thomas was only six years old. In 1635, when Thomas was 20 years old, he came to Virginia, claimed the land his father had left him, and built a new life in America.

The peace between the Indians and the colonists lasted five years after Pocahontas's death. On Good Friday morning, March 22, 1622, Indians gathered at the homes of colonists who had welcomed them during the Peace of Pocahontas. At a prearranged signal, the Indians killed many men, women, and children. More than a fourth of the colonists in Virginia died in a single day. Of the approximately 900 colonists who did survive the attack, half would be dead within the year from disease.

The Pierces

Captain William Pierce became Lieutenant Governor and Captain of James Towne, and served in one of the early General Assemblies of Virginia. Mistress Pierce remained the champion gardener of the colony. In 1620, three years after Rebecca died, John Rolfe married their daughter, Jane Pierce.

Captain Pierce, his family, and the others who lived in James Towne all survived the March 22, 1622, massacre, thanks to Chanco, an Indian who had become a Christian and lived with Richard Pace. When ordered to kill Captain Pace as part of the planned massacre, Chanco told Captain Pace of the plan. Captain Pace secured his own plantation, rowed across the river, and warned as many people as he could at nearby plantations. He arrived at James Towne just before daylight to warn the colonists there, all of whom survived the attack.

Temperance Flowerdew

Temperance met Captain George Yeardley, one of the Sea Venture passengers, before her return form James Towne to London. After another chance meeting with Captain Yeardley in London a few years later, they began to write to each other. In 1619, Temperance returned to Virginia as the wife of Governor George Yeardley.

Governor Yeardley held the first legislative assembly in Virginia and in America from July 30 to August 4, 1619. John Rolfe, secretary and recorder for the colony, attended the Assembly and served as a member of the Governor's Council. Reverend Bucke opened the Assembly in prayer. This first General Assembly addressed the need to establish families in Virginia: "In a new plantation, it is not known whether men or women be more necessary." In 1620, the Virginia Company agreed to send 90 young women to the colony. They very quickly became wives of the colonists.

Reverend Alexander Whitaker

Reverend Whitaker, well respected both in England and America, told his cousin in a letter dated June 18, 1614, that although his three years of service were over, he would continue to serve the spiritual needs of the colonists. Always close to his heart and ever present on his mind was his stated purpose for coming to Virginia: "that the Gospel may be powerful and effectual by me to the salvation of man and advancement of the Kingdom of Jesus Christ to whom, with the Father and the Holy Spirit, be all honor and glory forevermore."

Elizabeth Walton

Elizabeth never visited Abigail in Virginia. Although not permitted to attend the university herself, she did marry a college graduate from Oxford. She had three daughters and one son. She made sure her daughters were exposed to books of science, medicine, geography, and history, as well as literature. Elizabeth and Abigail continued their correspondence and shared their adventures and their friendship for many years.

Abigail Matthews

Abigail eventually married Robert Sparkes, once she was satisfied that Master Sparkes was no longer so impressed with himself. The first General Assembly in 1619 passed a law requiring each town to commit to the education, both academic and spiritual, of Indian children. The colonists planned to build a school that would prepare children, both Indian and English, for the college planned for Henricus. Because of Abigail's friendship with Pocahontas, several Powhatan parents were willing to let their children come to live with the Sparkeses to learn English and learn about the God of Pocahontas. Many hoped that what began with Pocahontas would continue long after her death. All that changed on March 22, 1622, five years and one day after she died. Abigail and Robert, who were visiting the Pierces in James Towne for Good Friday services on that fateful day, escaped the massacre.

The fighting that erupted between the colonists and the Indians as a result saddened Abigail greatly. Abigail Matthews, more than anyone, knew firsthand the power of forgiveness to forge eternal bonds of friendship between the most unlikely of peoples.

Now the Lord is Spirit; and where the Spirit of the Lord is, there is Liberty.
2 Corinthians 3:17

Dear Reader

When I wrote Liberty Letters I intended to communicate America's journey of freedom and also to illustrate the personal faith journey of girls who made bold choices to help others and in doing so, helped shape the course of history. Through their stories, we learn the facts, customs, lifestyles of days gone by, and so much more.

The girls I wrote about didn't consider themselves part of "history." Few people do. These were ordinary girls going about their lives when challenging times occurred in the communities in which they lived. They discovered integrity, courage, hope, and faith within themselves as they met these challenges with creativity and innovation. American history is steeped with just these kinds of people. These people embody liberty.

In *The Story of Pocahontas* I created the fictional characters of Abigail and Elizabeth as two friends who grew up together but whose lives took very different paths. Abigail's family chose adventure in the New World. Because of that choice, Abigail's life tested her character—sometimes severely—and caused her to look deep within herself for answers about courage, trust, and forgiveness.

Jamestown was founded in 1607, four hundred years ago. This is a long time ago, but archaeologists, through their research, have let us see a little of that time in history. In 1996, they discovered evidence of the actual fort of Jamestown, and then later on, found William Strachey's signet ring.

History books tell us that in 1613, Pocahontas was captured by the colonists, taught the ways of the English, became a Christian, and married John Rolfe. Do you ever wonder what happened to cause her to abandon her Indian heritage, renounce Ahone and Okee (her gods), decide to become a Christian, and then marry John Rolfe? If you look beneath a few lines in a history book, you'll find some great stories!

I did some digging of my own, not for archaeological artifacts, but to learn about Pocahontas, John Rolfe, Alexander Whitaker, and others. I read their letters, sermons, personal writings, and what others who lived during that time wrote about them. Then I asked this question: What if Abigail met Pocahontas? And that's how this story wrapped in historical events came about.

Your friend,

Nancy LeSourd

Pocahontas by George Edwards, circa 1910

THE WHITE FIGURE MOVED RAPIDLY

Pocahontas

Matoaka, or Little Snow Feather, was Pocahontas' secret tribal name. Pocahontas was born about 1595 and was the delight of her father, Chief Powhatan.

John Rolfe

John Rolfe, produced a valuable crop for Virginia. Tobacco, greatly desired by the English, was hated by King James I who called it "hurtful to the health of the whole body".

John Rolfe by Sidney E. King © The Jamestown Yorktown Foundation Collection, Williamsburg, Virginia

Their marriage in 1614 and well-known devotion to each other established the "Peace of Pocahontas" which lasted until 1622.

Recreated *Susan Constant* at Jamestown Settlement, Williamsburg, Virginia

Susan Constant

The *Susan Constant* is a replica of one of the first ships to arrive at James Towne in 1607. The colonists depended on ships like this one to bring supplies and news from England. An uneventful Atlantic crossing typically took between five and six weeks.

Settlers at James Towne and Henricus

Recreated Gardening at JamesTown Settlement, Williamsburg, Virginia

A settler at the reconstructed 1611 Cite of Henricus, Henricus Historical Park, Chesterfield, Virginia

James Towne Street
English Home, Indian Dwelling

mes Towne homes were built of sticks and mud called "wattle and ub" while the English lived in timber-framed houses. Later the lonists built houses of wood. Powhatan homes, made of mats and nt trees, provided watertight shelter.

Recreated early wattle and daub colonial houses at Jamestown Settlement, Williamsburg, Virginia

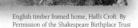

English timber framed home, Hall's Croft. By Permission of the Shakespeare Birthplace Trust

Recreated Powhatan Yehawken at Jamestown Settlement, Williamsburg, Virginia

Pocahontas and Son Thomas

This portrait of Pocahontas and her son, Thomas, may have been painted from sketches drawn of them while they were visiting John Rolfe's family in England in 1617.

Portrait of Pocahontas and Thomas. Unknown artist, circa 1800. Photo by David Pitcher with Permission of Borough Council of King's Lynn and West Norfolk

Regal Pocahontas

The Virginia Company stockholders wanted the English to know Pocahontas ("Lady Rebecca") as the daughter of the "king" of the Powhatans—a royal princess. She looks very English in her features in this painting.

Portrait of Pocahontas by Richard Norris Brooke ca 1905. Virginia Museum of Fine Arts, Richmond. Gift of John Barton Payne. Photo: Ron Jennings. © Virginia Museum of Fine Arts

Indian Attack

Colonists, desperate to find food during the Starvation Time, left the protection of the fort to forage for food nearby and were killed by Powhatan arrows.

Burial of the Dead During the Starving Time (Winter 1610) by Sidney King. National Park Service-Colonial National Historical Park

Burial of the Dead

The colonists buried those who died from starvation at night so they would not alert the Indians to their desperate situation.

Hornbook

Pocahontas probably learned to read and write using a hornbook like this one.

Secretarie Handwriting

Elizabeth and Abigail wrote to each other using quill pens in the flowing style known as "Secretarie" handwriting.

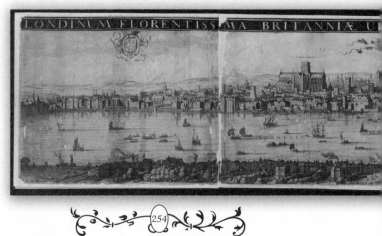